EVERYBODY'S

GOT

A

BILLY

A Collection of First-love Stories.

RITA H ROWE

Author's note:

While some of these stories are told true to form, the author has taken creative liberties with others to protect the identity of some of the contributors.

Copyright © 2023 Rita H Rowe

Love

First love

Sometimes forever love

Sometimes never love.

But always a someone you remember love.

This book is dedicated to my own Billy:
John, the one that didn't get away.

CONTENTS

EVERYBODY'S GOT A BILLY

Olivia and Nick – *Game, Set, Match*

"Sorry," she says as she puts a hand on his upper arm, straightening herself and glaring at Moesha, who gives her a guilty wave and snakes her way to the dance floor, quickly disappearing through the crowd.

"It's all good," he replies, noticing that her hand remains on his bicep. He flexes for a moment and when he sees the smile on her face, he blushes.

"My friend …"

"I'm Nick," he says and hopes she will stay rather than go in search of said friend.

"Olivia." She takes her hand off his arm and gives it to him. He raises it to his lips and kisses it, his eyes levelled at hers, his smile crooked, showing his interest.

She doesn't know how to respond. She feels tongue-tied. This doesn't happen often. She is a flight attendant, soon to be teacher. She deals with an assortment of people on a daily basis, many trying to vie for her attention. "So what do you do, Nick?"

"Studying to be a lawyer," he replies, without conceit. "But right now, I'm waiting for my buddy, who disappeared on me." She can't keep her eyes off his, and she notices him blush as he looks in the direction of the men's room. She takes the opportunity to size him up and she likes what she sees. Six foot something—perfect, because she needs a tall guy, someone who she can look up to when she kisses him, even in heels. Olive skin—compliments her own ivory tone nicely. Dark hair, shortish, a cute wave—would go with anything really but the contrast between those dark locks and her own blonde tinted hair ... She runs her tongue over her lips but he turns to her at that moment and she feels her cheeks go red.

"I have to go," he says and dashes through the crowd, hating to leave her but he has to. He is a responsible guy and his friend, Calvin, has probably drowned in the toilet. He hopes she will be there when he returns.

She waits. She wants to go back to Moesha, but doesn't want to leave this spot just in case he comes back. Oh, she likes him. A lot. There's something, she knows, but as she absently clicks the toe of her red heels to the beat of the music, she is becoming irritated. Where did he go? Did she seem too keen? She's never had to wait for anyone before. But he's worth it. She knows there's something there. Even in those few moments, she could feel it. No, she's not a waiter. She frowns. Maybe he is just a player. Maybe he is one of those guys who likes to be chatted up at nightclubs but likes to leave a girl hanging. No, she isn't going to put up with that. She's had that type before. At twenty-six, she's had enough of those. "To hell with him," she says out loud and heads back to Moesha, who has found some friends on the dance floor. She joins them, trying to put Nick, if that was even his name, out of her mind.

Nick is picking Calvin off the floor, cursing himself for letting him out of his sight. He should have taken him home, but if he had he wouldn't have met her. And he ran off like an idiot. He should have explained. Calvin had been in there too long; something could be wrong. He was already on his way to the toilets when she fell, literally, into him. But he can't get that gorgeous girl off his mind. He gently slaps Calvin's face and drags him, mumbling, to the wall where he props him up. Calvin promptly slides down to one side and Nick puts his shoulder under his friend's arm. He sits against the wall, his butt on the floor of the dirty toilet, Calvin's head rested on his shoulder, his snore bouncing into his ear. He can't leave him here, so he picks him up and takes him out of the toilet and drags him out of the nightclub into the fresh air. It's warm. He waits with him, watching people come into and leave the club. He hopes she hasn't left.

She has given up hope. He must have left. It's been over an hour and her feet are sore. She has tried to convince herself that he is not worth the trouble, but his face, his brown eyes that smiled into hers, making her feel like she was the only girl in existence, remains in her head. She's never felt so taken with someone. She's been in love before. She's had her heart broken before. But this. This felt different. Maybe it wasn't. Besides, he looked young, too young to be with her.

She heads to the smokers' area and lights up a cigarette. Moesha is still dancing, having found a guy who can shake it like she can. They will probably go home together. She looks at her watch. It's probably time she headed off too. She's getting tired. She smiles at other people out there and tries to avoid eye contact. Usually she is social, but right now, she can't be bothered being chatted up by drunk fellows who didn't manage to pick up anyone during the night. She's just about to put her smoke out and head back into the club when she sees him at the entrance. His head is moving about like he's searching.

For her?

She feels her heart lurch but holds herself steady. She's not about to get her hopes up again, but God, he's attractive. She throws down the cigarette and quickly lights another. She's not a heavy smoker by anyone's standards, but she wants to stay out here, let him find her. She looks the other way, her heart thudding in hope.

"Olivia," he says behind her.

She turns towards him and tries to look surprised, sound casual. "Oh, hi, Nick." It comes out as a croak and she clears her throat, embarrassed.

"I thought you might have left."

"I thought you did," she says, trying not to make it sound accusing.

"Sorry. My friend. He was passed out in the toilet."

"Where is he?" She looks behind him.

"I took him home."

"Oh." Her skin tingles. "And you came back?"

He smiles and dips his head, shy. "Yeah."

She needs to get this out of the way. "How old are you, Nick?"

"Twenty. Well, nearly twenty."

"Oh," she replies. She's disappointed. He's way too young for her. But … what does it matter? "I'm twenty-six," she says, looking for his reaction.

"An older woman," he says, his smile mischievous. "I like that."

There's an awkward silence.

"Tell me about yourself," she says, as he leans against the wall. He's getting comfortable. This makes her glad. She offers him a cigarette. He shakes his head.

"I've told you what I do," he says. "I'm a student."

"A law student," she says, raising her brows in admiration.

He looks down at the ground, self-conscious. "What about you? I mean, what do you do for fun?"

"I love sports. I play tennis ..." she says.

"No way! Me too," he says, his eyes lighting up.

She's emboldened. "I play competitively."

"Me too." He's off the wall now, leaning towards her.

"Are you having me on?" She's not sure he's not just indulging her.

"No, of course not." He's indignant. Why would he lie?

She laughs. "Well it sounds like a line."

"I don't play games," he says more seriously.

The attraction to him is getting stronger and she wants to reach out and touch his cheek. She looks at his lips, hoping to one day put hers on them. She relaxes. She feels comfortable with him. Everything around them seems to disappear.

He's looking at her, her green eyes that shine so brightly, looking at him like she wants him. Does she? Well, she wouldn't be standing here with him if she didn't.

"What else?" she says.

"What else what?" he replies, not sure of how to make this conversation last forever.

"Tell me about yourself."

He doesn't know what to tell. There's nothing that seems exciting. He's had a fairly ordinary life, a great family, whom he loves to death. He pictures her with them. She would fit in so well. They would love her. He just knows it. He hopes the age gap is not excuse enough for her to lose interest. But she's still here ... and he's getting way ahead of himself.

"And ..." She nods encouragingly.

"What's to tell? I study. I love soccer ..."

"Me too!" she says with more than a touch of excitement. This guy is too good to be true.

He laughs. "You're having me on."

"No. Why would I?" Now it's her turn to be indignant.

"My family would love you," he blurts.

"If they're anything like you, I would love them too." She's shocked that came out of her mouth.

He smiles. There's an awkward silence again.

"Are you seeing anyone?" he asks. Too upfront?

"No. You?"

"No."

Yet another awkward silence. He decides to keep to light conversation. He doesn't want to scare her off. "So, did you watch the match last Tuesday? Richard Gasquet, that French player with the amazing backhand? He's my favourite. I like to think I have a backhand like him." He lifts his chin proudly.

"Isn't he that left-hander? I watched him years ago." She narrows her eyes. She knows these things.

"No, he's definitely not a left-hander." Nick is a tennis expert; he wouldn't get these things wrong.

"No, I am certain he is a lefty …"

Nick is confident and wants to prove his expertise. He needs to impress her. "I'm more certain," he says. "Wanna bet?"

She's sure she's right. "Yes. Because I know I'm right." She's not so sure anymore. "What are we betting?"

"I win, you …" He looks upward, tapping his chin like he's thinking. He looks directly at her. "You kiss me."

He wasn't thinking at all, she knows. "And if I'm right?"

"Whatever you want," he says, hoping she wants the same reward.

"Okay. I'll decide when I win." She brings out her phone and googles. She's praying she's wrong. She wants him to kiss her so very badly. But she's also competitive so she's not sure she wants to be wrong. His head is over her shoulder, looking for the answer he knows they both want.

"Damn," she says and turns to find his lips so close to hers. She reaches forward and kisses him. She knows she is home.

****

Olivia and Nick were married seven years later. Age didn't matter. Nothing mattered but how they felt for each other and for both, a truer love they had never found. Nick has always been Olivia's Billy, no regrets. A match made in … well, you know.

Julia and Raj – *The Memento*

Yeah, he changed my life. Ten years together will do that.

I was a seventeen-year-old with not a lot going on in my life and he was a twenty-three-year-old, fresh off the boat from India, on the hunt for a wife.

I know. It sounds horrible and maybe I'm being horrible, still bitter, even after all this time. But I shouldn't be because I know he loved me. How can you stay with someone for that long without there being some love, some something …

How do I describe him? Well … I will begin with myself and then the comparison may be clearer. I am tall, for a woman; even as a young girl, I was taller than most girls my age. I am quite fair, being Australian, with bright-green eyes and dark wavy hair. I would say I was attractive; my friends called me beautiful, even though I never saw that. Raj was short, a few inches shorter than me, stocky, dark-skinned and dark eyes, but those eyes could mesmerise. I still get butterflies when I think about them, they were hypnotic …

Yep. I think that's the right word. I was hypnotised by him.

Of course, I was also an impressionable young girl, who sneaked out on a Saturday night to party at nightclubs, one of which we met at. I first noticed his smile. That smile, that just drew me in, just made me want to be around him and when he talked to me, I felt like I was the only person

9

in the world, not *woman*, but person. He had that way about him with everyone, I realised, but there was no denying the attraction the moment we lay eyes on each other. I don't think there was a need for coy flirtations or useless banter, we just came together and knew straight off the bat that we were going to be spending the whole evening together. We kissed that night, I gave him my number, as you did in the nineties, and when my friend Doris dragged me home, I wondered whether I would hear from him again.

He called the next morning and asked if I'd like to spend the Sunday in the Botanical Gardens. I did, and from that day on, it was assumed we were together, a couple. It was never stated officially; I mean, he didn't specifically ask me to be his girl, but I was. We spent every waking moment together, from the minute I got home from school, where I was completing Year Twelve, and he got home from university. He was on a study visa and so he was quite alone, finding company in a few mates from uni, who didn't really share his interests, except to go clubbing on a Saturday night. He missed his family, a million miles away in India, a close-knit bunch, that he saved money to call at least once a week and he wrote letters, endless letters to them.

At seventeen, I was living with my mother and had never introduced a boy to my family, but I brought Raj home very soon after and my mother welcomed him into our home, seeing in him what I did, a caring boy who was already falling for her daughter. They got along so well that at times I thought my mother loved him more than she did me! She saw what he did for me. From a fairly shy teenager, he brought me out of my shell, made me laugh, and as someone who had lived six years more than I had, took on the role of a sort of carer. He looked after me, looked out for me, made me feel loved, accepted, and as high school drew to a close, I knew he was my future. We had a similar outlook on life, similar values, as different as our cultures were, but he introduced me to Indian food, delicious flavours, and taught me how to cook exotic curries and tasty sweets. I, still a kid, really, didn't have too much to offer, except all the love I had in me.

I got along with his friends well, as he did with mine. It was a love story that I couldn't believe I had found even before I hit adulthood. We lived quite a long distance from each other and it was hard to see each other every day as we would have liked to, but we travelled by train or bus, as he didn't have a car and I didn't have a licence yet. When he could finally afford one, he taught me to drive, his extreme patience getting me through the frustrating lessons, but by the time we both had cars, we had already moved in together. I was eighteen by then and my mother gave us her blessing.

It was tough at first. I had begun working and he had a part-time job, so money was tight. But that didn't matter to us. In our little one-bedroom flat that sat atop five storeys of other identical flats, we spent time cooking and eating and watching TV from a black-and-white box that had been donated by a family friend. We welcomed guests, not caring what they thought of our tiny abode, for none of it mattered.

We were in love.

****

Six years of bliss. That's how I saw it; at least, that's how I remember it.

And then it wasn't. I will say, at this point, that perhaps the beginning of the end was my fault. All my fault. I was a twenty-three-year-old now, working at a bank, going out after work with colleagues, being invited out every weekend. Raj had completed his degree and was working in a coffee shop. Unfortunately, things were different then, even as recently as the nineties. No one wanted to hire a dark-skinned man as an engineer, even though he scored brilliantly in his degree. He was patient, the trait that kept him lighthearted, positive, hopeful. But I could see it grated on him, being passed up because of the colour of his skin. It helped when he was granted residency, because of my relationship with him; he felt like he was gaining ground on not being a second-class citizen and I was glad I could do something for him to make him feel better about his state of affairs.

By this time I was in a world of my own, being less excited to come home to Raj, who had the same stories of hope every day; how he was going to try to apply for different jobs while he regaled me with stories from the café in the city. It became boring. My new life, my new friends, similar in age to me, were becoming more interesting and when Raj showed disinterest in going out on a Saturday evening, I went without him.

I know, I know. Completely asking for trouble but I felt a bit trapped. Seeing my friends with tales of their weekends out, their evening coffees, the freedom they had that I felt I didn't made me resentful towards Raj and I found myself being irritated when the workday was done and I didn't anticipate the evenings with him as I used to.

I strayed.

I had gone to a club, the same club we had met just six years before, and I kissed another guy. I don't even remember what he looked like or what his name was for that matter. I went home with a sense of guilt but also a sense of freedom. Something that was mine, that I didn't want to share with him. It was exhilarating, new, fun. And the next weekend, I accepted the invitation from my friends and went out again. And again, I picked up some random guy.

I look back on it now and yes, it was a terrible thing to do, and there are no excuses, but I made them anyway. I was young when I met Raj and he was the only life I knew and as much as I loved him, I was curious. I wanted to know what else there was in the world. What was I missing out on? I hated myself, of course, despised my actions, knew better, and when he slept next to me at night, I stayed awake, staring at his peaceful face, contentment written all over it, and hated myself all over again.

The best of me finally materialised and I told him. There were no words from him and I don't want to describe the expression on his face but I knew it was over for us. I moved out of our flat, to a place that was closer to where I worked, and for the next two weeks, I cried myself raw. I knew what I had done. At the time, I regretted it, loathed myself for hurting him, but more selfishly, I was sad that I'd lost him. I knew he was the one for me and I had ruined something that could have been so wonderful.

You would think that's the end of this story. Unfortunately, and fortunately, it's not. It would have been simpler if it was. I would have mended my broken heart, he would have done the same. When Raj came over to return something, I think it was a CD or something as insignificant, we knew it was not done. We were in each other's arms, crying, kissing, and we ended up in bed and he left. And then every night, when he came over with one excuse or another, we did the same. He even came to see my mother, who had fallen ill, with me, and I found out later, he visited with her quite often.

For the next year, we were together almost every day. We didn't move back in together but we spent most nights and weekends together and I hoped that in time, it would all fall into place.

What I didn't expect was to fall pregnant. When I told him about it, his lips pursed. He wasn't so sure about it, didn't look terribly happy, but I knew I wanted this baby, with or without him. He stayed around, helped with cooking, massaged my ankles, cooked me special meals, some of which I fibbed were pregnancy cravings. I know he wasn't fooled but he wanted me to be comfortable, happy. We talked about the baby, what he or she would look like, how we would bring it up, where we would bring it up, but there was no sense of excitement from him, as much as I tried to make it seem like a new adventure lay ahead, that the next phase of our life was about to begin. By the end of the pregnancy, his visits declined. At this point I was dealing with my mother's illness and as such, I spent a lot of time at her house and I barely noticed he was not around very much.

When my son, Joshua, was born, Raj was not there and it made me angry but trying to push a nine-pound baby out of me was a distraction. I wasn't alone; my sister was there with me and I was just happy that someone was around, as my mother had passed away just a couple of weeks earlier.

Raj visited me at the hospital, bringing flowers and chocolates and a huge balloon and when I was released, he took me back to my place, cooked and helped with Joshua, always making sure we were comfortable and had what we needed.

But we were drifting as a couple. I didn't see it then, because I was so wrapped up in being a new mother, as I should have been, but I see it now. At that time, I just resented him not being around as much as I wanted him to be, to be a full-time father, to be of help to me. He told me he was working extra shifts to help with things financially, but I couldn't see anything extra coming my way. As contradictory as it sounds, I also didn't mind him not being around all the time. I wanted more time alone with my little boy and for the next two years, I had tunnel vision, not seeing anything apart from my son, watching him learn to crawl, walk, run, documenting everything for posterity.

One day I realised that it had been about a week without a visit or a phone call from Raj and when I tried to call him, there was no answer, so I decided to go over to his place to see if he was okay. The door was opened by one of his flatmates, who quite casually told me that Raj had gone to India to be married.

Married!

I couldn't quite register it for a while. I remember driving home, a numbness in my brain, and a hollering kid in the backseat of my car. Then, of course, for the next few days and weeks and months, I went through the range of emotions that go along with such a betrayal. Not one word had he said to me. I tried to remember the last time I saw him, if he'd mentioned anything, hinted even, but no, I guess I wasn't looking for anything, so I didn't see anything. I didn't notice him leave my life.

****

And what happened to Raj, I hear you ask. He was my Billy, my forever love. It turns out the woman he married was his Billy, his forever love, the one he left behind to seek a better future in another country.

Was Raj my forever guy then? Was he the one that got away? I don't think so. Or maybe. But he was my life when he was in it. Only until recently, I thought about him every single day. After all, the little boy growing up in front of me was the spitting image of his father. And for some reason, I had not given up hope of us all being a happy family; better late than never, right?

That hope ended when my then eighteen-year-old son decided to seek him out. I encouraged him to do so, helping locate him, knowing he was living somewhere in Melbourne. He did and when my son knocked on his door and was told by Raj's wife that Raj wasn't home, Joshua left his number and hoped there would be some contact.

Now, six years later, there's been none. The message is loud and clear. He didn't want any part of my son's life. How it affected Joshua, I don't fully know, but it was the point at which I began to hate him. And I knew it was over. Totally, completely over. I took off my rose-coloured glasses in defeat. I knew I would not see his smile again, his eyes light up at the sight of me, his loving words whispered in my ear. It was done.

Raj has found happiness; at least sometimes, I hope he is happy. He was a perfect partner to me for a long time, but he was never a father to my son. I think the worst part of it all was that I felt like a pawn. Someone he used to get his residency so he could bring *his* forever love into the country and raise his own family here.

And me? At forty-six years old, I finally found my love, quite soon after I went through the grief of Raj's absolute absence. Paul is his name, and there is a love born of togetherness, a give and take. I adore him and he makes my heart full.

But will I forget the man who first had my heart? I cannot. I see the same eyes, the same smile every time I look into the face of my boy, the memento left by a man who I once loved.

Anthony and Regina – *First, Last, Everything*

This is a short story. A long road but a short story. Not that it isn't interesting in the journey, but who wants to hear about happy people? That's just boring, so I've tried to keep it short and sweet with the promise that love, yes, true love, does exist.

There was a girl, a young woman, who had her heart broken. Who thought she would never forget her Billy. The boy who made her laugh, the boy who made her grow up, the boy who betrayed her. And Anthony was supposed to be the rebound guy, the one who was to temporarily take her mind off who should have been her Billy.

I was just nineteen. At university, studying to be a nurse. No interest in nursing really, but just enjoying the ride as university students sometimes do, spending most of my spare time with friends at the bar, playing pool, or watching other people play pool. I spent some Saturday evenings at nightclubs with my best friend, sometimes meeting interesting young men, who didn't keep my interest very long. I thought my heart still belonged to another, who had just viciously broken it once again.

Then came Anthony. Spanish, dark hair, olive skin, green eyes that you couldn't really tell were green because of his hooded eyebrows. He was handsome, there was no doubt, but I was tentative about taking steps with him.

You have to understand the backstory of Anthony. I went to school with Anthony, two years my senior, a friend of my brother, Nev, not a close friend, just someone who played basketball with him sometimes. Now Anthony's sister, Mary, was a beautiful girl, but somewhat snobby, and walked around with her nose in the air, most of the time on her own. I never warmed to her and there was no reason to. And I had no idea she was related to Anthony either.

One night at a club, I saw Anthony and Mary dancing with a few people. My friend Danni and myself joined their group and I found myself wondering if the two of them, Anthony and Mary, were a couple, even though they didn't seem to be. I was jealous, I realised, but concluded that if this guy was unavailable, well, weren't all the good ones taken?

It was in the ladies' room that I discovered the connection, as Mary and I talked while we fiddled with our make-up, and I felt relief sweep through me. It was then that I realised that my relief was because I was attracted to Anthony, that he had made me notice him. Mary, on the other hand, was quite different to what I perceived her to be at high school; however, it had been a few years before and perhaps she had grown out of her strangeness. Mary and I exchanged phone numbers and we continued our night. I left the club hoping I would see Anthony again.

I didn't call Mary and she didn't call either and I thought, well, that was that. Maybe the excitement of the night caused us to get overenthusiastic about becoming friends. But one afternoon, while walking back home from uni, I felt a dejection about the state of my life. I was nineteen, had a good social life, was not really interested in the course I was completing. I had just had an argument with my father the night before about how much I was going out and I was a little over being treated like a child, having to explain my whereabouts while every other person my age seemed to have the freedom to do what they wanted.

It may have been a premonition, a feeling, a sign from above, but I remember thinking to myself as I plucked out Mary's number from the bottom of my handbag, *this may change my life*. I snickered at my idiocy but when I got home, I went straight to the phone and dialled.

Mary and I became great friends. I soon discovered her parents were almost as strict as my father and she was not allowed to go out without Anthony accompanying her. Which is why they were at the club together. But as I got to know their parents, they began to trust me and allowed her to spend time at my place as I spent time at theirs. Anthony was around sometimes but during the day when he worked I missed his presence. He was shy, spoke little, but I found him glance in my direction more than once and found myself more and more attracted to him. The three of us all went out to the clubs together often and danced all night. I was having a ball.

One evening, a few weeks later, Anthony and Mary were supposed to pick me up on the way out. Only Anthony appeared and off we went. We had a good time, dancing together and flirting and when he dropped me home, he kissed me. I was just tickled that he felt the same way about me and I found myself thinking about him all the time. After that it was assumed we were together, and his family, who seemed to know it was coming, were just as pleased.

Now, I'm an overthinker and a couple of weeks later, my thoughts got the better of me. I knew Anthony's heart was not one to be trifled with. I wasn't sure I could give him all of mine yet and a fling was not his thing. He was a serious man, a one-woman guy. I wasn't sure if I was that woman and I didn't want to lead him on anymore and end up hurting him.

So I broke up with him. He was subdued; he may have been angry but it was his sad face I couldn't get out of my mind when I returned home. And all I did was think of him. What was I waiting for? This was the serious relationship I'd wanted. He was everything I had ever asked for in a man, handed to me on a silver platter and here I was second-guessing this gift. But I needed to ponder it, I needed to make sure I wouldn't break his heart and if we spent any more time together it would be worse. I had been in love before; it didn't end well and I couldn't be the one to hurt someone the way I had been hurt. He would get over me. He would find someone else who wouldn't break his heart.

Two days. That's all it took to realise the mistake I'd made and I was back at his place, in his arms, kissing him, telling him I was all in if he was. We were inseparable after that. We spent a lot of time together and sometimes even dropped Mary at the club as she still wasn't allowed to go on her own, and went off on our own. One evening, we had fallen asleep in his car and returned to the club to find it closed; Mary, accompanied by a bouncer, stood in front of it, her face thunderous. We apologised through stifled laughter, and took her home.

It was a few weeks later when I had a massive argument with my father. I still didn't have the guts to tell him about Anthony and he never knew that I had the slightest interest in boys. It was odd because any nineteen-year-old should. I don't remember what the argument was about, I think it may have been about going out and I didn't want to lose Anthony. I knew I was already in love with him, not even a few weeks after our first kiss. So I left home, did the cowardly thing, ran. In the middle of the day while my father was at work, I bundled my clothes in a bedsheet and went to live with my sister. Oh, I cried, for what I'd done, for how I hurt my father but at the time, it was the only way I knew how to get my freedom. And Anthony supported what I did. He didn't agree with it, but he stuck by me, accepting every decision I made, bad or good. I continued with my studies as much as I didn't want to, and spent every evening with the man I loved.

One evening, I was sitting on Anthony's lap. We had been out to the movies the night before, some picture about a wedding and the topic came up. It was too soon, of course. It was a day shy of a month of being together as girlfriend and boyfriend. But I thought I would tease him. "So, when are you going to ask me to marry you?" I kissed his cheek and laughed at my audacity.

"How about now?" he replied and adjusted me on his lap to reach into his pocket and take out a black velvet box.

I sprang off his lap and covered my mouth with my hands and he smiled and got on one knee. "Marry me?" He opened the box and pulled out a garnet set on a gold band. "I wanted to get you something nicer ..."

"That's the best ring ever," I said and put out my left hand. "Yes!"

The rest is history. We were wed a year later. There were naysayers, doubters, but we didn't care. The quicker we got to spend our lives together the better. There were times we could barely wait for the wedding, wanting to elope before the day, to know we belonged completely to each other, but we didn't. We waited and got married on a beautiful day in July, and danced our first dance to 'The Wonder of You' by Elvis Presley.

Eleven months later, our first daughter was born and in the next few years our second daughter and our son. For the next thirty years, we lived in bliss. Oh, there were ups and downs, for how can something so true not have them? Our children are grown, wonderful human beings who could sometimes run us ragged, but we did it all together.

I did tell you this was not going to be a crazy story, fraught with drama, which there was at times, but ultimately, it is a true love story. Working together towards a common goal, in it until the end. I would die for him and I hope I die with him, for what would life be without this man by my side?

Oh yes, did I tell you that I dedicate every one of my books to him?

Eliza and Pete - *Doomed From Day Dot*

You know, most people think that the crazy love, the one that you would die for, the one that would ruin you, happens when you're a teenager, when you're impressionable. That love, the one you remember fondly. The one you think that maybe it would have worked out if you were just more mature, did things differently.

Pete and I met when we were both twenty-three years old. Older than mad teenagers, but the maturity part, well … We had a lot in common, that was for sure. We were both veterinary nurses at an animal sanctuary, so our love for all things paws was the first thing we found attractive about each other. Maybe not the first thing.

I have to describe him, what I saw when I first walked into that office when he was putting a puppy into a crate. He was on his haunches and even though I was nervous, being shown around by my new manager, Bree, I stole a second look. So when Bree asked me to wait in the reception area to retrieve some papers, I took the chance. Why, I didn't know. His back was to me. But then he turned around and I knew I was gone. Those eyes, piercing blue, bore through me and there was complete silence, like the world had stopped still for this moment. Destiny?

"This way, Eliza," Bree was saying.

He ran his fingers through his hair and stepped forward, putting out his hand eagerly to me. "Pete," he said. "Welcome." His teeth flashed through his widely parted lips and I just took his hand, my jaw dropping slightly. I was as confident as any girl could be, but he just put me off-kilter, had me floundering for a moment before I got back my bearings, flashing him just as toothy a grin.

I went home that evening with Pete still in my head. I hadn't seen him for the rest of the day and believe me, I had searched. My eyes had darted this way and that all through the tour I was given by Bree, but to no avail. When I put my key into the front door, I tried to clear my head but I could hear sounds coming from the kitchen.

Jase was already home. Jason, my partner, the one I thought was going to be my true love.

"Hi, honey," said Jase, pecking me on the cheek. "Haven't started dinner yet. Can't wait to hear about the new job."

"It's fine. I'll have a shower and we can do it together."

I let the pins of water beat at me and scolded myself for my stupid attraction to some guy who I had barely said a hello to. And out there, preparing dinner for me, was Jase, my high school sweetheart, who I had given five years of my life to. Maybe it was just stale with Jase. We'd been living together for two years and the excitement of it had all but worn off. I was waiting for a ring that never seemed to materialise and he was obsessed with his job as an accountant, making plans to relocate to Sydney. It sounded exciting but I was not sure I wanted to leave my life in Melbourne behind, my family, my friends, my new job … The run-of-the-mill life I'd dreamed about with Jase had too quickly run its course. We were different, wanted different things in life and even though I wasn't clear why then, I think I was a little over succumbing to what he always wanted to do. But no excuses for what came next.

I towelled my wet hair with more gusto than I usually did. I was angry with myself for my thoughts. Sure, Pete was attractive, but it wasn't like I was planning on doing anything stupid. It was healthy to have attractions to other people and Jase was a good-looking guy, so I'd never really cared about looking at anyone else. Why was I making a big thing in my head about someone I'd just taken one glance at?

I put Pete out of my head, enjoyed dinner with Jase and went to bed, letting the image of him flash before my eyes before I fell asleep. And the next morning, after Jase left for work, I spent just a little extra time on my make-up.

I fell for Pete hard. It was immediate and intense, and by our interactions, I could see he felt the same. I worked beside him the next day, cleaning out an enclosure. He was fun, outgoing, sexy and his smile, it turned me to dust. He had a big family and so did I, we enjoyed the same music and the same films and sometimes we talked about nothing in particular but we always seemed to be on the same page. There was a connection, a magnetism, but my heart fell when he told me he was married—just seven months, a newlywed.

I felt a stab of animosity for someone I'd never met, completely forgetting the fact that I was in a long-term relationship myself. Jase and I had been friends for a while before we began dating and even though I had always had a strong attraction to him, nothing had prepared me for the bolt of lightning that hit when I met Pete. I know how it sounds, like something from a movie or a novel, but nothing I had seen or read had knocked me about like this. I went home from work every day more confused than the last.

Each morning I woke up with a spring in my step and on the weekends I was despondent, counting the minutes until Monday morning. I tried not to think about him but it was becoming impossible and as the days turned into weeks and the weeks into months, we became closer, confiding in each other about issues with family, friends. Whenever anything bothered me or I had something of importance going on in my life, the first one I wanted to share it with was Pete.

At work we sought each other out, waiting tentatively each morning for the day's tasks to be assigned and when we were not scheduled for duties together, my shoulders drooped and when I looked towards Pete, his demeanour mirrored mine.

One day, after the morning briefing, he walked past me and paused. "Do you want to get a coffee at break?" I nodded, feeling a thrill of anticipation. He grinned. "Good. Meet me at my car at eleven."

We began to go out together for lunch every day and sometimes stopped at a bar for a drink on the way home from work.

"What about your wife?" I plucked up the courage to ask one evening as we sat at a table in the pub. I wanted to know where his marriage stood. It was clear that he was attracted to me. He took every opportunity to be near me, every excuse to brush against me 'accidentally'.

"Mel is ..." He paused and shrugged. "We've been together since I was sixteen. We were married even before we were married. It was an expectation ..."

"Do you love her?" I butted in boldly.

"I care about her very much." He narrowed his eyes at me. "What about you? Your partner, what's his name?"

"Jason," I replied and fiddled with my glass. I didn't want to talk about Jase, which was unfair since I had brought up the topic of our respective partners. "We've been together for a few years …"

"Do you love him?"

I nodded, dreading the fact that it might put him off. "I do." I said. "But it's a different sort of love now, you know," I quickly added, hating myself for diminishing my relationship with Jase. Yet it was going downhill, I had to admit. Our relationship, I now saw, seemed more and more one of convenience. He was interstate a lot, and when he was in town, we didn't spend a lot of time together. I would like to put it all on me, take the complete blame for it, but I realised later that Jase and I had emotionally left each other long before we physically parted.

Ed Sheeran's 'Perfect' was playing in the dim bar and Pete took my hand and I upturned my palm, entwining my fingers in his. I let myself feel the music, get lost in the romance of it all. All I could see in front of me was Pete and this song that was playing seemed like it was written for us. We talked a bit more, but I don't know what it was about, my chest hurting from the tightness I felt, my skin tingling from his touch. I didn't want to go home, I didn't want this moment to end but it was getting late. He walked me back to my car, his hand still in mine, and when I opened my door, he leaned in and kissed me.

****

We spent a year together, Pete and me. A beautiful, tumultuous year.

After we kissed that night, I had to salvage whatever respect I had for myself and break it off with Jase. He took it badly, perhaps not so much because he was losing me, but more because of my betrayal. I didn't blame him, I would have felt the same, and strangely enough, in time, we became friends, really good friends, which is what we had been to begin with. I still have so much love and respect for him that he put aside his hurt and forgave me.

Pete, on the other hand, found it hard to let go of Mel. "She's unstable," he said, a few months in. He seemed reluctant to let her go and I was starting to wonder about his inability to leave his wife.

"She's better off knowing though. What are you waiting for?"

"Just give me some time," he replied.

I was a little irked by his inability to be upfront with her. After all, I had broken up with Jase to be with him. But I tried to understand. They had been together a long time and of course it would be a terrible thing to do. But it did make things a little difficult for us, finding the time and opportunity to be together. It irritated me that while I lay alone in bed in my apartment, he was in bed with his wife.

But working together was fun; spending time together after work was wonderful. With Pete and I, it wasn't just a physical passion, it was a meeting of the minds. We enjoyed doing things together. Like getting coffee, playing basketball, going for walks, especially the moonlight strolls on the beach where we would hold hands and I could believe that we were a real couple. There were the late night drives, catch-ups in secret at my house or after work before heading home, going to the drive-in, playing video games together. The best times were when he stayed over late; what alibi he gave his wife, I didn't know, but we'd watch TV or listen to music lying in bed, his arms wrapped around me, and it was the closest I ever felt to pure happiness, the closest thing to perfection I felt with a man. Just being in his presence made me feel whole, alive, vibrant.

It sounds like a ridiculous contradiction, loving him like that, but it felt wrong. I couldn't quite put my finger on it. Perhaps it was the obvious—he was still in the process of working out how to tell his wife about us and I felt like the other woman. Well, I was the other woman, the mistress, if you will. Let's call a spade a spade. But it was the loneliness of being without him when he was not around. My mind was constantly on him, an obsessive habit that was grating on my nerves. I wasn't usually the type to be so obsessed with someone. I was an independent woman, who actually liked having time by myself. But I was living alone, which I had never done before, and as much as I tried to busy myself with going to the gym, playing soccer, spending time with my family and friends, nothing ever filled the void of going to sleep in a big empty bed knowing the person you love is sleeping next to somebody else.

So I tried to end it. And again. And again. I'd send him a message saying I couldn't do it anymore, that I was done. And he kept luring me back in, telling me that he was going to do it, leave his wife or at least tell her about us and give her the opportunity to leave him. At the time, I guess it was what I was hoping for, so I let myself believe that he would. I didn't really want to let go, so I held out hope that we would be together, completely together soon.

"It's over," he announced one evening with a flourish. He had with him a bottle of wine when I opened the door, and I threw my arms around him, hoping that finally our life together was about to begin.

We made love that night but as I lay in bed, his warm body next to mine, something about it felt wrong. We had spent a joyous evening drinking and listening to music and laughing. Laughing! That was it. He had just broken up with the woman he had loved for so long and there was no regret, no remorse, no inkling of sorrow. Even if he was happy that we could finally be together out in the open, did he not have a care for how she was feeling? A little bit of compassion? Far be it from me to remind him to feel this way, but it just felt, I don't know, not right. I tried to put it out of my mind and enjoy him, be happy with him.

But something changed. Almost immediately.

In retrospect, I think he didn't quite know how to deal with it. She had been his childhood sweetheart and he didn't know life without her. It was like a switch was flipped. He became jealous with me, obsessive, and overbearing. And on the other hand, he was out and about, without me, drinking and partying with friends, coming back to my place late at night, sometimes not, preferring to stay at his own place, a rental flat a half-hour drive from my place. I understood. That he needed to have his own space, that it would be jumping the gun for us to move in together immediately, but I guess I assumed that we would be spending most nights together. Isn't this what we had hoped for, dreamed about?

We stayed together for four more months after he left his wife, but our relationship wasn't the same. We fought constantly. I was still playing second fiddle to his ex-wife. He was still in contact with her and it peeved me. It shouldn't have, I know. The better part of me should have won out, but when he told me he resented me for how he hurt her, I was angry. Soon after, his wife tried to take her own life and the guilt overwhelmed him ... and me. It became worse when I received a message from him telling me she was going to kill herself. I didn't know what to do, how to respond to that. So he was back at her place every couple of days, trying to sate her. She manipulated him and in turn, he manipulated me. I struggled to be with him at that time, trying to let go, but I couldn't do it. I wanted, no, needed him in my life. I loved him completely.

Not many people knew about us and my family and friends were not fond of him or the idea of him. They had liked Jase and were quite sad when our relationship had ended. So it was hard to talk to anyone about Pete, how things were with him. I looked like a fool and I didn't want to hear "I told you so". I turned to Bree, my manager, who was well aware of what had been going on the whole time. She allowed me to wallow but I couldn't tell her the extent of my feelings. I was too guarded, too mixed-up.

I was weary of it all though. Something had to give. And it came in the form of suspicion. At first, I tried to ignore the pictures on Instagram, Pete with his arm around another girl amid a group of friends. A friend, I told myself. I had lots of male friends too. I didn't expect him to be suspicious over them. So I chose not to ask him about it, to be the bigger person. After all, he had given up his wife for me, I kept telling myself over and over. Why would he seek female companionship elsewhere when he got what he wanted?

But I couldn't ignore the other evidence that cropped up.

Toothbrushes that weren't mine in the cabinet under the sink in his bathroom, mine along with them. "Tim and Jack left them there," he explained with a shrug.

Make-up on his bed sheets, that didn't come from my face. "Has to be yours." He narrowed his eyes at me. "I've seen it on your bed all the time too." I knew that it wasn't mine but I didn't know how to counter that.

Empty bottles of wine that sat atop the rubbish bin, lipstick stains on the rim. I knew he didn't drink wine. "Friends," he said with defiance. "I had people over last night."

Every suspicion I had, he had an answer for, not really seeming to care if I believed him or not and each time I saw him, I left fuming, ready to end it. Inevitably he would message me to come over and as angry and even humiliated as I was, he managed to convince me to stay.

Then finally, one evening, standing in the middle of a main road, arguing after a night out, I had had it. He was still talking about some girl we had been chatting with at the bar we'd just left.

"She was pretty hot, don't you think?" he said, as if he really expected a response from me.

I had been trying to ignore his behaviour before we had left, the way he leaned into the buxom blonde when he spoke, whispered something in her ear that made her giggle. "Yes, I'm sure she is," I replied. Then I stopped. "You know what, Pete?" He stopped at the tone of my voice. "Go back there. Go back to her. I'm done."

"Eliza, don't be silly," he said, and put his arm around my shoulder.

"Leave me alone," I screamed, and shrugged his arm off with such gusto that he stumbled backwards and landed in the middle of the road, a car screeching to a halt metres in front of him.

I put my hands to my mouth in horror and he just sat there on his butt, looking at me in bewilderment.

"Eliza," he called and got to his feet, but once I saw that there was no damage, no injury to him, I bolted, away from him, out of his life.

I quit my job, dumped all his things outside his flat and tried to erase him from my mind. Two weeks later, I found out he was dating Bree, my now ex-manager. It was funny, odd, really, since she was the first one to know about my relationship with Pete, the one friend I had at the sanctuary who I trusted with my secret. Bree, the one who gave me advice and a shoulder to cry on when things began to fall apart. Well, I guess she was preparing to pick up the pieces after I left. Needless to say, I have also forgone that friendship.

I thought of Pete often at first; when a song we enjoyed together came on the radio or when mutual friends would talk of him, my heart would race. I thought for a while that he was my forever guy, that I would never love anyone like that again. But I realised that he was toxic, his charisma was a front for his insecurity. I knew I couldn't go back because I could never trust him again.

I had believed Pete to have been my soulmate. When we first met I physically felt an electric shock run from my head to toes and through my stomach by just looking at him. I thought at first our similar tastes in everything only stamped that illusion. And the chemistry, oh, there was an abundance of that. Both of us agreed that perhaps we met at the wrong time of our lives but I think it was something that had to happen for me. Infatuation runs thin when there is so much at stake and I learned to look out for the things that really matter, the real meat of a relationship— reliability, empathy, security and support. Pete may have been the one that got away, but I'm so glad that he did and I don't ever regret the relationship, as poisonous as it was. I think it was more like me dodging a bullet and remembering the trajectory, it taught me how to avoid the signs of bad love and eventually led me to my true better half.

It's been three years. I met the love of my life, the one who values and loves me and who I respect and love in return. It was difficult to accept that I could be loved like that again and my thoughts returned to Pete often. I knew my relationship with Pete was never going to end well. It didn't begin well. It was based on lies and deceit and I knew that I was as much at fault as he was, but I loved him with a fury that I never knew I had.

We saw each other at a party some years later, Pete and me. I was fearful of how I would feel, what our interactions would be after such a long hiatus. Would my heart still jump when I saw him? How would it affect the beautiful relationship I was in now, if it did?

"Hi, Eliza," he said after wriggling his way through the crowd towards me.

"Hi, Pete," I replied and let him kiss my cheek. My heart burst out of my chest. All I wanted to do was go home to the man I was in love with. I had no inclination to stay and bask in his presence as I once did. I knew I was not under his spell anymore. I could move on. "Bye, Pete," I said, and turned and walked out the door.

Oh, and his wife; well, she moved on as well. I guess she dodged that bullet too.

Jack and Priya - *We Were Eleven*

Only eleven years old when I felt the sudden urge to ask her to be my girlfriend.

Before that, we were simply great friends and whenever we'd spoken, it was only kindness and laughter on that sweet face with dancing eyes.

She said no at first and walked away with a confused expression and I just stood there, looking down at my shoes, a broken-hearted eleven-year-old. For about five minutes. Because then she thought about it and ran back to me said yes.

We spent every lunchtime together, had inside jokes as you would, and back then, holding hands was the equivalent of a lover's kiss.

We were dramatically torn apart through the Year Seven school migration and although I was sad to leave her when I moved to another school, I thought that I'd meet many others just like her and have many other relationships and the same feelings.

So I made the call. I squawked into the phone, when her very strict Indian father answered, pretending to be her best friend and when the phone was passed over to her, I told her that it wasn't going to work. We had to end it because we'd never be able to see each other. She agreed, reiterating the same fact. We were of the same mind and it made me feel better about the whole thing.

****

But there was something there and I've never been able to put my finger on it. I'd see her, at the shopping centre, at the movies, and I'd feel something. I had other little school crushes, went out with girls who didn't stir much in me. But this one affected me.

Then, a few years later, she began part-time work at a restaurant that my family and I frequented. I'd walk in, say hi and she would smile slightly, her eyes lowering in nervousness, and I'd always feel a quickening of my heart. I'd go home and get on Instagram, where I would find that the boy whose initials she usually had on her bio would disappear, and I'd find myself smiling stupidly into my phone. And then it would reappear and a dank feeling would run over me again.

But it seemed like whenever I went into the restaurant, and then checked her Instagram, the same thing would happen again and again. It couldn't have been a coincidence. I'd hear my parents say they were going to pick up dinner from the restaurant and I'd pretend I didn't want to go, when really, I was slapping on hair gel and spraying on tons of deodorant. As if she was going to smell it from across the kitchen over the spicy aroma of Portuguese chicken.

One night, I followed my father into the restaurant to pick up dinner. He spoke to her, asking for the order and paying for it and unbeknownst to him, we were both sneaking glances at each other, secret smiles. My father grabbed the bag of food and walked out in front of me but as I turned around to shoot her a grin, the door rocked back and slammed into my shoulder, just missing my nose. But I wasn't concerned about the pain; I turned around quickly and caught her giggling. Not the 'that's weird' giggle but more of the 'that's funny — he got distracted by me' kind of giggle. I wasn't even embarrassed; in fact, I'm glad it happened. I saw her smile directly at me. I saw her look into my eyes. And I knew we felt the same thing. I went home that night and my brain didn't waste time thinking about anything else. I'm quite sure I was smiling during the car ride home too. I didn't even care if my father noticed and thought it was odd. She was perfection and I wasn't afraid to admit it to myself or anyone else.

Adulthood arrived for us both. We didn't see much of each other for a while and I never really questioned why we never contacted each other. I think the timing was off: I was trapped in a petty relationship for a while and when I was single before that, she'd had somebody.

One day — I was twenty-one years old now and at my cousin's twenty-first birthday party — who did I see? Yes, she was there. I knew they were friends, or at least acquaintances, but I was surprised to learn that they were living together, roommates in another state, Queensland, just the two of them, all on their own, so far away from everyone. I wondered about the connection, they hadn't even gone to the same school, but I didn't think about it for too long, because I found myself fixated on her from that moment on.

Thoughts of her invaded my mind, day after day, night after night. I was in a serious relationship, completely in love with my partner, so this was an odd feeling and I didn't quite know how to deal with it. I suddenly started to question if I was truly happy or heading down the right path because how could I be thinking about some girl from Year Six when I was in a steady relationship with a beautiful woman and a bright future? It didn't make sense and the more I thought about her, the more the guilt I felt began to eat at me. It was as if I had cheated on my girlfriend when I had barely said a word to her. My saving grace was that she was so far out of reach, having gone back to Queensland after the party.

A few weeks went by and I tried to be patient, assuming these thoughts would simply disappear in time. But they only worsened. I couldn't understand why the thought of her caught such a strong hold on my brain. And then suddenly, there she was again. At the grocery store, while I was shopping with my partner. She looked me dead in the eye and I looked away, feeling my heart drop to the floor. My nerves spiked so heavily that my face became blotchy and I started babbling, so much so that my partner thought I was sick and I was glad when she dragged me out of the store. I had even more guilt, and began to believe that my thoughts of her manifested her appearance.

It seemed to me now that it might be a spiritual connection I felt with her, a meant-to-be sort of thing, and I wondered if I'd ever popped into *her* head. Maybe she had been thinking about me too and there we were, in the same place at the same time. And suddenly, she was everywhere—at a shopping plaza packed with people, in a restaurant at a crowded table; I'd find her eyes through the throngs of people and just know there was still something there. And then she wasn't. She'd disappeared again and I realised that she'd gone back to Queensland. I don't know if I felt relief or grief.

Soon it began affecting my relationship which is where I knew the line had to be drawn. I unintentionally put stress on my partner because of how I was feeling. It wasn't fair. How could I act the same with my partner as I usually did when my mind was occupied by another woman? My partner began to suspect something was wrong but how could I begin to explain a situation like this to her? It would have destroyed us.

In the midst of all this and knowing my head wasn't straight, my partner was nothing but supportive and generous, which only made me feel more guilty and confused. I thought about it, trying to weigh up my feelings, sort them out somehow. What would I be giving up? This person who was so pure, kind and loving. I couldn't do that to her. I couldn't hurt her. She was everything I'd ever wanted. Why would I do this to us?

And yet, I still couldn't steer clear of the fact: I was obsessed with another woman.

Maybe I was making it out to be a bigger deal than it was?

Maybe I hadn't crossed her mind with great thought since Year Six?

Maybe her smile was so kind and inviting that other men made the same mistake, too?

I began to think that this was God's way of telling me she's my soulmate, especially with all those strange coincidences and incidents. We even seemed to have so much in common. Yes, I even checked her online playlists and she listened to the very same artists that I did — specific artists, uncommon music, which most of my friends and family would never have heard of. It was as if these playlists were tailored for just her and me.

I imagined holding her hand, I imagined playing with her hair, I imagined exploring countries and destinations with her. Was it possible to be addicted to the thought of a human being? It must be because it can be all-consuming at times.

I imagined meeting her family. I imagined telling them the wonderfully spectacular story of us finding our way to each other after ten, long years. I imagined talking to her sisters and giving them advice on love. I even dreamed of sharing Christmas and holidays together.

I'd built an entire life with her ... in my head.

Oh shit, was I stalking her? Did that count as stalking? No. I'm not some guy in a trench coat crouching behind a bush with binoculars. Maybe it was all in my head. But she was there for a reason. Something was feeding me these thoughts to tell me something, maybe. This couldn't just be me grasping at straws.

The feelings for her weren't even in the slightest bit sexual; in fact, I wish I could have blamed it on hormones. At least then, I'd have some kind of explanation, some kind of answer.

Maybe it was only a one-way street?

Maybe she did think of me but knew it was impossible because I was the one in a relationship?

Maybe I felt I had unfinished business over an unnatural break-up? Even if it was only in Year Six.

My conscience was filled with guilt, but also love, thinking someday we'd be together. I had the urge to throw my life away for her, even picturing scenarios where I'd talk to her about my current relationship in past tense. Which again led to more guilt, which I guess I deserved.

Should I have simplified my life? Dumbed it down to society's expectation? Married somebody, anybody adequate. Buy a house, have children: be comfortable. That's all that matters, right?

Why couldn't I think that way like most others? Or was my brain sabotaging me and trying to tell me I didn't deserve what I had or didn't deserve to be happy?

Nobody ever told me how complicated these things could get.

Maybe we were together in a past life?

Maybe we'll be together in the next life?

Maybe she was the one that got away?

Or better yet, the one that never was ...

She was just so happy. At least, she looked it all the time, every photo of her and every time I saw her. Her soul was a bright one, I could tell. Maybe that's what it was that drew me to her? Her positive energy and cheerful aura. Or maybe I was used to looking at pictures of her where by default, everyone's going to look happy in pictures, right? But even that opened up the door to the possibility of her having bad days—God, I'd want to be there to make those days better, I'd want to be her shoulder to cry on, her home, her sanctuary.

But what if we did end up together? Was her bright outlook on life going to rub off on me? Would I finally be happy? Or would it work the other way? Would my negative energy affect her persona? Would I ruin her? Maybe she was better off without me and that was why our stars weren't aligning?

Who knows? Maybe I'd put her so high up on this goddamned pedestal that if anything ever did happen, I was going to be disappointed. She'd probably be completely different and I probably wouldn't like her at all ... Or was that just my way of making myself feel better about not actually ending up with her?

I'd love to tell you we ended up together. I'd love to tell you she's mine. Turns out she's now in a relationship. She looks happy. I hope she is. He's lucky and I hope he knows that and treats her how I would have. I wish I could tell you I learned something but really, I just forced myself into confusion and now I remain with lingering fractures in my brain. Maybe if we're meant to be together, it will happen on its own ... maybe someday.

Did my own actions force us apart? Is my only way of knowing going to start by leaving the person I'm with? Do I really love the person I'm with? Or are my views of my partner being poisoned by this fake sense of spiritual fate found in another woman who, deep down, I don't even know ... We hadn't even had a real conversation since Year Six.

Maybe we were just kids and this all means nothing?

After all, we were eleven.

David and Elizabeth - *Opposites Attract*

Attraction was there, no doubt about it. Blonde, cascading hair that fell over one shoulder, blue eyes, not the colour of the shallow water that hovers near the beach, but a deep blue, almost green, encircled with dark curled eyelashes, and her mouth, oh, when she smiled, those white teeth, gleaming with confidence! Was it a put-off that she knew how she looked, how people stared at her? No, not to me. The self-assurance with which she carried herself was an utter turn-on. This was a girl, no, a woman, who knew what she wanted; none of that 'take care of me' rubbish about her.

We were both in university in London, she in her second year of accounting and I was just beginning my year of teacher training. We were at a bar, out with our mutual friend Roxy, and I knew I wanted Elizabeth right off the bat, even when she leaned into me, slurring her words and batting those eyelashes.

"Hi, stranger." For a petite twenty-year-old, she could throw down a truckload of alcohol, more than I could to keep up, but I grinned at her devil-may-care manner and reached out my hand in greeting. She looked down at my outstretched offering and suppressed a giggle. I should have been offended, but I was intrigued.

"Hello," I replied.

"Elizabeth, gotta go," came Roxy's voice.

"But," I began to protest but Elizabeth was already waving me goodbye with a pout as Roxy pulled her off the barstool. I scowled at Roxy who pretended not to notice as she dragged Elizabeth out of the bar. I turned back to my beer and took a slug, a smile plastered on my face and hers emblazoned in my brain.

Yet another Friday, yet another tough week and I sat at the same bar, on the same barstool, hoping the year would fly by. I was sick of studying. If anything was going to get me by more quickly, it was keeping busy. I was contemplating going home after just an hour, perhaps hitting the books, getting a head start on my assignments but Peter, one of my classmates, had other ideas. I hoped he was done chatting up every pair of legs that walked into the bar.

"Hi, stranger," a voice behind me sung as I ordered another beer.

An unexpected jolt went through me. I knew it was her even before I turned around and I felt the ends of my lips curl in pleasure. "Hello. Elizabeth."

"You remembered my name?" She pulled up a stool beside me and wiggled her bum into it. "I thought you were too drunk to remember that night."

"I could say the same," I replied and wondered if that were the right thing to say. Usually I was a confident guy, not really caring about what people thought. A take-me-or-leave-me sort of man, probably as most twenty-one-year-olds are when they begin a new phase of life; you know, slightly cocky. But here I was, wondering if I had offended this girl by what I'd said and it took me a little by surprise.

But she laughed, her head thrown back slightly, and put her hand on my shoulder. "Touché," she said and signalled for the bartender. "By yourself?"

"No, just waiting for my mate, Peter." I gestured to the men's room. I hoped now that Peter would take his time. "You?"

"Here with Roxy. You know Roxy, don't you?" I looked over to Roxy and waved, hoping that Roxy would not take it as a cue to approach us. I hoped we could just chat together, alone, sober.

We chatted, about what I don't completely recall as I was too busy soaking in her aura, her presence, the way she laughed at my stupid one-liners, the way her brows knotted when I was telling her something serious, again, what, I don't remember, but I got the feeling she liked me. I don't know what it is, how you can tell, but you can tell. There was an attraction there, certainly on my part and I was pretty sure it was mutual.

"Elizabeth, David," I heard and we turned to see Roxy signalling us over to a table. We both turned to each other, disappointment in our faces. But through the evening, we knew some spark had been lit. The sly catching of eyes, the coy smiles, the looks between us that told each other we wished that it were just us, alone. Everyone else at the loud laughing table was a blur. But when she suddenly got up to leave without even a glance in my direction, I thought I had imagined the whole attraction thing and was disappointed in myself. I was a young guy, sure, who could misconstrue signs, but maybe I was just seeing what I wanted to see. I went home a little disheartened but nevertheless, I was not one to give up easily on something, so the next day, I called Roxy and asked for Elizabeth's number.

"She's taken, buddy," said Roxy, and after we exchanged a couple of words about the night before, I hung up the phone and breathed a deep sigh of sorrow, or maybe relief. I decided to close the book on this very short chapter, the romance that never was.

Months went by and Elizabeth would pop into my head at times and I hoped that we would bump into each other again, but I didn't dwell on her; she was unavailable and I wasn't going to crash a party at which I didn't belong. However, one evening after a boozy night out with Roxy, I decided to see where things stood and I asked her for Elizabeth's number.

"Why?" Roxy screwed up her nose.

"Because I would like to call her, maybe invite her out for a drink or dinner or something."

"You two are very different, you know." Roxy looked at me, slightly perplexed.

"Maybe. But opposites attract," I said, flashing a smile.

"Not always," replied Roxy, her head dropping.

"Well, is she still with that guy?" I pressed. Roxy shrugged. "Come on, Rox," I said, knowing she was weakening. I'd like to think I can be quite persuasive, especially with six beers bloating my belly.

"No, she's not with him anymore," said Roxy and began striding away from me. Then she turned around. "I'll text you her number," she said quietly and I watched her walk away. In hindsight, I realised the reason for Roxy's hesitation; she wanted me for herself. I wish I had been more sensitive, but what would I have done anyway? I had no feelings of that kind for Roxy, as cute and sweet as she was.

I sent Elizabeth a text the very next day. *Are you single yet?*

Maybe, came the reply and I smiled into the phone. I'm as cluey as the next guy, which is not saying much, but I decided to take that as a yes. So, with my confidence high, I asked her if she'd like to meet up and she agreed.

I was trying not to get my hopes too high, but the moment I saw her, I knew there was a connection, just like the last couple of times I'd seen her all those months ago. We talked as we sipped on our drinks, hers vodka, mine a beer; we talked about family, friends, what we did for fun, and I realised how dissimilar our lives were, not that it deterred me. Elizabeth was from a wealthy family, a staunchly religious one, and I was from a working-class family, who struggled to get by. She was fun and flirtatious, enjoyed the fact that she turned heads, while pretending not to notice, and I was as down-to-earth as one can get; well, I'd like to think so anyway. But she laughed a lot, enjoyed my sense of humour and I began to relax in her presence. She touched my arm each time she threw her head back in laughter and I wanted her to keep her hand on me. But I was not someone who threw myself at a girl and this one, I wanted to have for more than one evening.

"I live just a couple of blocks away," said Elizabeth with a twinkle in her eye. "Want to take it back to my place?"

I was elated. Not that I was going to take advantage of her, I was just relieved that she trusted me so soon. "Sure," I replied and we walked to her flat, her arm entwined in mine.

"Wow," I blurted as I walked in, looking around at the spacious room, the plush sofa, the wall furnishings, the shag carpet. "How do you afford all this?"

She shrugged. "My father pays for it," she said, nonchalant.

"Why?" Stupid question but it just came out.

"Because he can," she said with a laugh. "Another beer?"

"How about coffee?"

She pouted affectedly. "Okay."

"So, you're a rich girl ..." I teased.

She paused and leaned her shoulder against the wall, tilting her head and narrowing her eyes. "Is that going to be a problem?"

I was taken aback by the question. "No."

"Well, you know that pub we were just at?" I nodded. "My parents own it. And six others around London." My mouth turned into an O and she laughed. "I don't care about all that shit," she said. "I'm going to make it on my own stead." I loved the way she talked, a little posh, but the way she enunciated her words was nice.

We stayed up all night talking, continuing our banter from the pub, and before we knew it, the morning sun was making its way through her chiffon curtains. "Wow," I said. "That went quickly. I have to get ready for school. Going to be hard without much sleep."

"Not just for you," she said, her voice tinged with disappointment.

She walked me to the door and we stood facing each other for a moment. Then I took her in my arms and felt hers go around my neck. Her mouth was soft, gentle, but demanding and I had to pull back first for fear of her getting the wrong idea. "See you soon," I said, trying not to smile too happily, and walked back to my own flat, quite a distance by foot, but I was happy to stroll all the way, taking in the night before, trying to relive every second of what was an amazing night.

****

Elizabeth and I were inseparable after that night. I took her to a fancy restaurant that usually had a waiting list of at least a few weeks, but with the help of a friend, I managed to book a table there the next evening. I spent most of my savings to eat at a place that served a little blotch of green on a very large plate, and left hungry, but Elizabeth looked like she belonged there, like she spent a lot of her time in fancy restaurants. After that we went back to her place and this time we didn't wait to kiss each other. The moment we were in the door, her lips were on mine, and I hungrily explored her face, her neck ... We didn't make love that night; oh, I wanted to, but as we were getting hot and heavy, she whispered to me that it would be her first time, and I couldn't do it. We played around, we kissed, we cuddled, talked and laughed some more.

It wasn't specifically labelled as such but we became an item. We spent most of our spare time together, and although we didn't have a lot in common, just being together was the most important thing. A few weeks later, I was at her parents' house for the weekend, a lavish country ranch on a large piece of land, green as far as the eye could see. Her parents were good with me, her mother made me feel welcome immediately but her father, well, fathers are always a bit wary, aren't they? Elizabeth was clearly

Daddy's girl and he was making sure I was good enough for her.

"A teacher?" he said, pursing his lips, when I told him about my plans for my future. At this, Elizabeth lowered her head and I was a little surprised that she hadn't jumped in to defend my choice of career even though I knew how she felt about it; she was always trying to tell me that I was destined for something bigger, something more. For me, what was more noble than helping to carve out the paths of future generations? I hoped in time it was something she would come to understand, and that her family would accept. I didn't realise it then, but it was the first of the cracks that began to appear in our relationship.

We were expected to sleep in separate bedrooms, but by now, Elizabeth and I had already made love, yet it was exhilarating and dangerous when she sneaked into my bedroom, a middle finger up to her father's ideals. She loved being the rebel, even though she was a secret rebel, not wanting to upset the applecart of her perfect family life. It was clear by now she was spoilt, got everything she wanted, but that didn't diminish my love for her, and by now I knew that I loved her. Like I had never loved anyone before.

Our romance continued as it had when we got back to London. We went out drinking, went to parties, out for walks, read together, laughed and loved together. But our differences, as much as we tried to ignore them, were creeping out of the woodwork, the most contentious issue, my lack of ambition. I couldn't understand it really; I wanted to do what I loved doing and being a teacher was not a career to be scoffed at. I tried to argue my point on many an occasion but I tried to see her point of view. I could understand that in comparison to her parents' wealth, her upbringing, that what I would make as a teacher would not keep her in the lap of luxury, the lifestyle to which she was accustomed, but to me, all that meant nothing. Unfortunately, to her it meant a lot, especially when the reality of a life together was becoming a real possibility. There were other arguments too, friends, domestic issues like leaving out the milk or some other innocuous incident, which we chose to see as getting used to each other, little things that we both let go of easily.

So it came out of the blue. A poem, which she read to me as we sat on the grass in the park one evening, one that she wrote. I can't remember the exact words but well, it was a break-up poem, a sad little sonnet that expressed her sorrow at having to leave me. No real reason; she loved me, but it was never going to work.

I had no words. I was choked up, unbelieving, not sure of what was happening, or what had happened to bring this on, but I certainly wasn't going to stand there and beg for a more detailed explanation. I turned my back on her and walked away. I still had my pride and I was damned if I was going to let her see me shed even one tear.

If that was love, then I didn't know what pain was. The tightness in my chest, the way my jaw hurt when I discovered my teeth were clenched, the difficulty to hold back a sob ... But I held my head high, tried not to think about it too much and my friends rallied, kept me busy, kept me drunk through it while I tried to think I was a stronger man, one who could easily flick the pain off my cuff, get over her. When three months went by without a word, I thought I was making headway when fate, or whatever you want to call it, laughed at me.

"Hey, stranger."

I was back at the pub with my friends, not the bar her father owned, another one close to my flat. My heart flipped and I turned to see Elizabeth standing there, that same flirty smile on her face, and before I could reply, her lips were on my cheek. I didn't know what to say, how to say anything, but I felt an anger bubble up in me. I don't know what it was, perhaps her indifference towards what had happened, her greeting me like nothing had happened. Maybe I just hadn't stopped to process the break-up, her reason for leaving me. But I smiled and gestured to the seat beside me, which she took, and we chatted like we were old friends, all the while, my heart beating so hard I thought she may be able to hear it. When she left, I sat there alone with my empty glass and felt relief. I had held back my anger, treated her like a friend. Maybe this was what they called closure. I sighed. No, I knew I wasn't over her. I wondered if it showed and she knew my composure was an act. She seemed to know me so well when we had been together.

We bumped into each other a few times after that and with each time, it became easier to talk to her, but I knew I had to keep my distance, even though she flirted outrageously with me. I didn't want to be drawn into her life again and I wasn't sure where I stood with her. She had broken my heart and I was not going to go through that again.

It was nearing the end of the school year and Elizabeth called me. She wanted to meet up and I agreed, unsure of why. I went to her place, tentative at first, but we were soon laughing and talking and it felt almost the same as the first time we had come to her place together. We talked about her plans for the summer, her trip to Mexico and I told her of my summer job at a school and I was glad we had the chance to talk. This meeting felt like closure even though no mention was made of our relationship or the break-up and I still had too much pride to demand an answer. The urge to kiss her was strong, but I didn't and after a night of chatting and listening to music, I left, this time without the kiss and felt good about the whole thing.

This was it, she wanted no more from me and I was confident I felt the same way or would do so in time.

I went back to my life, met a lovely girl, Laura, whom I had a lot in common with, maybe not the connection I had with Elizabeth, but she did a lot to help me move on and I thought I had made strides in my attempt to rid Elizabeth from my head. I'd even planned to travel the world, Australia to begin with, to broaden my horizons, to see things before I settled anywhere.

Unfortunately, when the summer had ended, Elizabeth called again and invited me out for a drink. For some reason I couldn't resist and I met with her and as usual we ended up back at her place, but this time one thing led to another and we found ourselves in bed together. It was one of the best nights of my life and as she lay beside me, a gentle snore escaping her parted lips, I knew it was her I was in love with. She opened her eyes and put her hands over her eyes.

"Stop staring at me," she said as I removed her hands from her face.

"You're beautiful," I said.

"Let's be together, David." She sat up and grabbed my fingers, squeezing them. "I've never loved anyone like I loved you. I missed you so much, I can't think about life without you by my side."

I had questions, of course. Why did you leave me? What have you been doing all this time? More importantly, who with? Who was it that you loved? But I didn't ask them. Right now, I didn't want her to reconsider. I knew I was weak when it came to her and I didn't care. There was still so much I wanted to share with her, for her to share with me. She was aloof, that was a given, but I was determined to break the exterior and find the real woman in there, the vulnerable human that I knew deep down she had to be.

"Well?"

"We are going in different directions, Elizabeth," I said.

"I know." She pouted. "You're off to Bournemouth, to your school." She emphasised the word *school* like it was a vile expression, but I ignored the implication. I nodded. "We could try long distance," she said suddenly, her eyes shining. "And it's not too far. Only a couple of hours away. We could see each other on weekends?" This was what I wanted to hear. That she wanted to try no matter what, no matter how hard. That I was worth the effort.

"It's only for a few months," I said and then I knew I had to tell her of my plans — to travel to Australia. I had been saving for this trip since she had left me and I wasn't about to put it off. I hoped this wasn't a dealbreaker but she had to know.

She listened, nodding, smiling, and I could see her brain working from the way she bit her lip. "You know what?" she said when I was done. "What if I join you? When I've finished uni, I could meet you there and we could go about together, you know, be a couple of gypsies." There was an edge of excitement to her voice which was contagious and although I never fathomed for a moment this would be an option, I was pleased. It could work. All of it.

It did work. For a while, at least, it did, the thrill of a new job keeping me busy enough not to miss Elizabeth too much and the craving for her being sated on the weekends when she came up to see me in Bournemouth or I came to London to see her. When I left for Australia, I missed her like crazy but the thought that she would soon be with me, experiencing this life with me, kept me energised, excited. And I loved the place, the idea of getting to see what I had dreamed of. I wanted to stay here, create a life here, one I hoped Elizabeth would be part of.

She met me in Cairns and we travelled around Australia together but by the time we left for India, which we had decided we both wanted to do, we were arguing all the time. Little irritations, major decisions, marriage, children, all the topics that couples have, all of them ending up in differences of opinion. She had quite a temper, but admittedly, so did I, and I was certainly not going to constantly defend my life choices to her all the time. But our love for each other always won out and we let things go. Which, in hindsight, was not a good thing and even though I could see that we were drifting apart, there was nothing I could do to stop it.

When we got back to London, it was all but over. I got a job in a school, not a great one, but a job nevertheless, where I was unhappy and we spent our time together barely talking because when it came down to it, I felt like nothing when I was with her. I went out almost every evening, usually without her, and drowned my sorrows at the pub, knowing that something had to give.

Eventually, Elizabeth ended it, via a text message, but by that time, I didn't care about how. A poem, a text message, what was the difference: a break-up was a break-up and this time, I was done too. This was it. When I went to her place to collect my things, two weeks later, she had them ready for me at the door. Without a word I grabbed the rubbish bag and as I walked away, I stopped to take one last look at her but she was inside, the door already closed on me. I dropped my head in disappointment that we had nothing more to say to each other, but as my eyes fell on the stoop, I saw a pair of men's boots sitting there. I took in a deep breath. I knew who she was when I met her. She would never be alone.

I packed up and left for Australia, knowing I needed a clean break, a different life, a place where I wouldn't be made to feel like I was worth nothing. I haven't looked back. I found a good job here, made my life here, I met my wife here, and the rest, as they say, is history.

Why is Elizabeth the one that got away for me? She's not really. I'm glad she got away, I'm glad I got away from her, literally having to leave the country to be rid of her. But I loved her deeply, my first real heartbreak, the first one I thought I could spend the rest of my life with. The one who could drive me insane but I loved so hard. There is never the matter of what if. I tried. We both tried. We were just so different and we thought we could beat those odds.

We couldn't.

Anna and Freddie - *(Un) Closure*

I nearly gave it all up for him. Twice. But no one ever made me feel so mad, so beautiful, so crazy in love.

I met Freddie when I was in high school. If you ask me, or either of us, for that matter, who our high school sweetheart was, we would without a doubt say each other. We had other boyfriends, girlfriends, even during our high school years, but there was just something that brought us back to each other. Connection is a banal word, chemistry, too mysterious, magnetism ... maybe. But different, absolutely.

He was a sports fanatic. I was studious. He was fair, blue eyes and blonde-tipped hair, I was olive-skinned, brown eyes, dark wavy hair. He had freedom, just like every other Australian male, I had an Italian father who was as strict as they come. He hung around in the cool group, who didn't have much interest in studying but played sport, I was on the outer edges, my head in books, my extracurricular activities that included the school play and reading. We were chalk and cheese. But gosh we loved each other.

I didn't really know he existed until I was dating one of his friends, a cool, handsome guy who resembled Leonardo DiCaprio, a heartbreaker. But Freddie was different, he stood at the edges of his super-cool group. When I was unceremoniously dumped by the ruthless Mr DiCaprio, I was heartbroken, thinking I had lost my first love. I had no inkling of what love was, but there was Freddie, ready to pick up the pieces of my broken heart and put them back together.

I didn't realise I would fall in love with him, not with the superficial sentiment I had for Leonardo, but with a fierce love that bordered on obsession. When he was not with me, I was an empty shell, waiting, counting the minutes until I saw him again. When I was in his arms, I was home, but there was still the feeling that I needed to be closer, like I needed to become a part of him.

Even though I was still only seventeen, I gave myself to him, something I never regretted. I always wanted my first time to be with someone I loved. It was, of course, like most first sexual experiences, painful and awkward, but after that ... well. We enjoyed learning, exploring, loving, growing together into adulthood and I couldn't imagine being with anyone else.

Life always gets in the way and for us, this was no exception; most high school romances come to an end. We didn't need to wonder what went wrong. The list was long. He wanted freedom to be with his friends, I wanted only him. He wanted me whenever he wanted me, my freedom was limited. He was crazy jealous when another guy even talked to me. I was the same. We fought. And we fought. We were tired of fighting. He was tired of it more than I was. So he ended it.

That was not the end. For the next three years, through university, through our busy social lives that sometimes included each other and at other times didn't, we always came back to each other. He ruined relationships for me that may have gone somewhere, I ruined the same for him. It was an addiction for us, the inability to let go completely, an inexplicable magnetism. It was a weakness that was hard to overcome and at the time, it was harmless as we were not hurting anyone else but also toxic because our fighting never stopped. Something drastic needed to happen for it to be over completely.

Her name was Shelby. One of my best friends, who wormed her way into my group, with her sad stories of mistreatment at the hands of her father. Of course I looked out for her. She needed love; she needed me. Turned out she needed more than my love. After a weekend away with my friends, something which I was not a part of, as at nineteen, I still wasn't allowed to go away for a camping trip with my friends, Freddie announced that he was seeing Shelby.

I can't quite describe the feeling; in fact, I think I don't remember quite clearly how it actually felt when he told me, his eyes on the floor, his shoulders slumped as he stood in the aisle of the supermarket for which he worked part-time. We had hurt each other a lot during our time together, but this was a betrayal of magnificence. The enormity of it didn't register until I was at home some hours later, when I found my pillow soaked with my tears. That's when I knew something had to give. I had to stop loving him. I knew it was a choice. I would not be a doormat and this revolving door of love and hurt had to be locked. I sat up on my bed, pulled out all mementos that I had collected of and from Freddie in the last few years, put them all in a bag, and literally threw him into the dumpster and out of my life.

I knew I could do it, rid him from my life. And I did. When I began to think of him, a habit that was hugely ingrained in my everyday life, I would banish the thought of him, instead finding something to distract me. It worked. The little niggle in my heart began to stop nudging and without realising it, I was free.

Good timing. Because not long after that, I met the love of my life, the man I would love with every fibre of my being, the one I would literally die for. Paul was like no man I had ever met. Kind, strong, handsome to boot. And he loved me like no one ever had. I had never felt so safe, so happy. When he asked me to marry him less than a year later, I accepted. I wasn't letting this one get away. And another kind of love formed in me, one born of passion, but also of respect, self-love, tenderness and shared goals. We had children: two girls, beautiful, self-confident, loving, caring. We built our life on love. We were not rich, we struggled, but we finally found our feet with our careers, mine as an accountant and him as the owner of a gardening franchise. We were different too, but we always found common ground. And there were jealousies, but we never fought. We worked it out with talking, loving, caring for our little family.

What happened to Freddie? Well, here was the problem ...

I saw Freddie a few times. The first time was in a shopping centre about four years after the fateful incident. I was shopping for Christmas presents for my family and when he asked if we could have a cup of coffee together, I agreed, ignoring the massive thump in my heart upon setting eyes on him again. He told me how much he hated himself for what he did, how Shelby was nothing, a distraction, a selfish, hurtful thing that he regretted the moment it happened. There were tears from both of us, but I forgave him.

"If you hadn't done what you did," I said with a smile, "I wouldn't have found the love of my life."

"I'm just so sorry." He looked so sad.

"I'm happy, Freddie." I said. "So all is well. There's nothing to be sorry about." I looked at my watch. "I have to go get the girls from their grandparents' house."

He walked me to the door of my car and with a kiss on my cheek, I got into my car and watched as he walked back into the shopping centre.

My heart was beating fast, so fast, and I looked at my reflection in the rear-view mirror. My eyes were a little red and I took a deep breath. I touched the spot on my cheek that his lips had grazed, still feeling the burn of his skin on mine. I was affected. More than I realised I would be. I slumped in my seat and cried, ugly cried. Tears that cascaded down my face, snot that dripped out of my nose. I heaved with a passion I had thought I'd never have for him again. It was my grief. That which I had never come to terms with. The betrayal of it all, I hadn't really felt until this moment. And I let it all out in that carpark, oblivious to the people rushing around me doing their Christmas shopping. Then I wiped my face with the rest of the tissues, noting I would now have to replace the box. After all, I was a good mother, a good wife. The tears streamed down again. I went home with my chest heavy but puffed out. Closure, I called it.

There was no closure.

He didn't leave my head. As much as I wanted to get him out again, he didn't go. I went through the motions of life for the next few days, trying to maintain a semblance of normalcy for the sake of my children and the man whom I completely loved, guilt filling me every time I looked at him. I rued the moment I bumped into Freddie. I began to rue the moment I even met Freddie. I even rued my tryst with Leonardo for leading me to Freddie.

In time it waned, the emotion, and I was confident I could be the person I was before I set foot into that damned shopping centre. But thoughts of him crept into my brain, when I was alone, which, when you have two toddlers, isn't that often, so that was my saving grace.

I bumped into him a number of times during the years, at a friend's place, at the same shopping centre, but trusting the strength of my marriage, I didn't let my emotions after seeing him put doubt in my heart. I thought it probably would always be like that forever. After all, everyone has a first love, someone who will always have a little part of their heart, memories that would completely be theirs. I got used to him entering my head every now and then and I was okay with that.

An email. That's all it took. So simple, so benign, yet so lethal.

I don't know what made me do it. I hadn't heard from him in years. I had been in touch with him a few times via email over the years. A greeting for his birthday, a congratulations on his wedding, another congratulations on the birth of his children, twins. Nothing too complicated, just a curiosity about his life, his about mine.

But this was different. Maybe it was the time — the girls were nearly adults, had lives of their own, the man I was married to, I still loved fiercely and life was, in fact, more than perfect. And maybe that was it. It was a self-sabotaging act of defiance. I was tired of being everybody's perfect. I wanted to be bad, to be selfish, have something that was mine, that I didn't have to share with my family and friends.

And let's face it, I wanted answers. For something that had happened more than twenty years before. I had forgiven, or so I thought at the time, but I hadn't forgotten.

So I emailed Freddie. The last time I had seen him was a few years before on a street with his twin girls, adorable little toddlers that were the spitting image of him. I had the same reaction as I always did: I let myself think about him for a little while, had feelings of nostalgia, resentment and sadness, brushed them off and then moved on. But for some reason, I couldn't get him out of my mind lately. I needed to know. With everything I'd achieved in my life, I still wanted to know why he'd done what he'd done.

So I asked him. In an email. After the pleasantries, I asked the question. "Why? Why Shelby?"

A reply came forth in a couple of days, days that I bit on my shellacked nails, cursing myself for my impulsivity. "I was stupid," he wrote.

"Not good enough," I wrote back.

"The one regret in my life, the stupidest mistake I made, was her."

"Why?"

"Because I lost you forever."

I cried then, tears I promised myself I would never shed over him again. But they flooded out of me and as disappointed in myself as I was, something about how he wrote it felt like regret, like he was sorry I was out of his life. But it still wasn't a satisfactory answer. I wanted him to say that he was sick of the steps we had been dancing together for so long, the back and forth, the jealousy, the fights. That he got together with Shelby because he knew it would be the nail in our coffin. Of course it was, but I wanted him to have a good reason for what he did.

But a mistake? Which meant that I was never a part of the equation.

That he did what he did because he felt something for her. Which devastated me.

That I was so insignificant to him at the time, that his part in it all was just a thoughtless act, a 'mistake'.

I replied, telling him it was fine, it was a good thing that it happened or else I may have still been pining for him if it didn't happen, that my life turned out wonderfully because of it. It didn't escape me that I was pining as I wrote. We discussed our lives, our successful careers, his as a veterinarian, our children, a back and forth that became more personal with each email.

"I loved you like no other," I wrote.

"You were my true love," he wrote back.

It became an everyday conversation: 'How are you?'; 'What are you doing today?'. No mention of our respective partners. It was easier to avoid the topic than confront what was now becoming more than friendly banter.

"We should have coffee," he suggested one day.

"You may not like what you see," I responded. Time changes things, adds things to one's face, body, and even though I was as confident as a forty-something-year-old could be, the thought of seeing his disappointed face was unbearable.

We met for coffee in the city on my lunch hour, convincing ourselves that we were two old friends catching up, but it was still there, the chemistry, that connection. I wanted to touch his hand, which twitched with the nearness of mine. His eyes, still so blue, so beautiful. I wanted to reach across the table and kiss him. I didn't. We flirted, talked about life. Then I asked him about his wife. Was he happy? He shook his head.

"Not so much," he said.

I don't quite remember my initial reaction to that. Was I happy because he wasn't? Or was I disappointed that he was only interested in me because he wasn't happy? I was still yearning for him despite my own satisfaction in my marriage. He asked about mine and I told him the truth. I was happy. I didn't elaborate. I don't know why. Perhaps it was because I didn't want him to leave me alone, that if he knew my marriage was a loving, affectionate one, he would do the honourable thing and back off.

He walked me to my car after the shortest hour of my life, and hugged me goodbye for a moment longer than was necessary, me not wanting to let go of the familiarity of his embrace, the scent of him, which I kept trying to savour as I drove back to work.

When I checked my email, a message was already in my inbox. "You are still my baby. And still as sexy as ever," he wrote. I burst out in laughter, the tension of the meeting pouring out of me, the relief that his attraction to me was still there.

We continued our conversations, each one becoming more open, more dangerous. But it wasn't long before I realised that I was in love with him again. And I hated myself for it. I hated him for it. I argued with him over email. I brought back things from the past, things that happened as teenagers, Shelby.

I needed to see him again, but we both knew a coffee this time would not suffice. There were things to say to each other, explain in person, real 'closure', whatever that meant. We met at a carpark and I got into his car. Not a second had gone by when his lips were on mine. Then we both pulled apart and laughed, a nervous giggle. But another minute later and we were in each other's arms again. The feel of his lips on mine, it was like time had stood still. They felt the same, tasted the same, it was like I was transported back to that reckless sixteen-year-old.

"This is insane," I said.

"It is," he agreed, trying hard to keep the smile from his face.

I took his hand and entwined my fingers in his. "I don't know if I can forget what you did," I said, feeling the tears already welling.

"Don't cry, please. Don't cry for me." He wiped away the tears that dripped down my face. I looked up at him and saw anguish in his eyes, a pain that he felt for me, his eyes wetting as I stared into them. I knew he hated himself for what he'd done. For something so small, so insignificant, that could have the repercussions it did.

The first time in that car, we kissed, we cried, we held hands and when I left him, I was lost, not sure I would ever see him again, and determined not to.

For what was I doing? Was I about to show the same disrespect for the man who had breathed love back into my lungs, gave me hope of happiness, not just hope, but happiness itself? Was I about to throw everything I loved away, for someone who once had my heart and trampled on it? Guilt overtook me. I was erratic; I was ending it with Freddie one minute and starting it again. For his part, Freddie was just as torn. We needed to talk again, I said. Set things straight about this roller-coaster I never thought I would get on again.

We met again, in the carpark. We kissed, with abandon, like we had been doing it forever, passion just as strong; no, stronger than there was before. "We need to talk about our partners," I said when we finally tore our lips away from each other's. He looked like that was the last thing in the world he wanted to talk about but I was unwavering. It had been two months and it was the topic we had skirted around. "You first," I said.

"Mine is … complicated," he said.

"Can you talk about it?"

"She's a good mother, a great person, but we are friends. There's nothing there, hasn't been for a long time."

"Is that why you're here with me?"

"No," he said and squeezed my hand that was already in his. "You, I've never felt like this with anyone. Not anyone."

I lowered my head. I couldn't say the same. But I needed to be clear with him. "I will never leave Paul," I said, tears welling at the thought of hurting the man who was my life. "I would take a bullet for him. I will die with him. He is my life."

There was a short silence in which we both kept our eyes off each other. "Then why are you here?" he asked.

"See, there's the point," I replied, turning to his forlorn face. "You are here because something is missing in your life. I'm here despite the love I have for my husband."

"But if you're so happy …"

"I don't know," I cried, really not knowing, not understanding. "Maybe it's a midlife crisis," I said and broke into a sputtering laugh. He pulled my head to his chest and I let it stay there, feeling the rise and fall of his chest, feeling like this was what I had truly missed.

The next few months were spent in much the same routine. We met nearly every week, kissing, touching, holding, talking. And life at home remained the status quo. I didn't love my husband any less. I spent time with him, went away with him, made love, great love, with him. But I still couldn't give up Freddie. Some part of me couldn't let him go, as much as I tried. I tried fighting, I tried reasoning, being logical about the situation: he could never leave his two children, become a part-time father, and I could never leave my husband and the life I had built for myself. But it could not go on forever. Freddie was patient with me, he didn't fight with me as he used to, which for some reason annoyed me. To me, it was him not caring, which I couldn't bear to face. Maybe he had finally grown up. I clearly had not.

I despised myself, rightly so, as this went against everything I believed in, trusted, everything I had instilled in my children. But I was back to being that teenage girl who loved Freddie so ferociously, she was willing to risk it all. He was in my head from the moment I woke until I put my head back on that pillow. An all-consuming obsession that I had now learned to disguise. Tears in the shower, a smile that hid my desperation when I wasn't with him, talking with people, conversations that I barely heard, hardly remembering what I had said. A nervous energy held my body for all of those eight months until I knew it had to stop. I was going insane, destroying the life I had been so blessed with. I became determined to break it off. I had tried a number of times already via email.

"We can't go on," I'd write.

"We should stop," he'd write back.

We didn't.

"We have to end this. I can't do this anymore, not to the people I love."

"If this is affecting you so badly, then I understand. But I will take you however I can have you," he wrote back. "Even if it's a check-in to say hello every now and then."

"You know we can't just do that."

"I understand. But I can't let you go."

There were times I felt I could let him go, when I felt strong, when I was busy, when other parts of my life kept me moving. I thought, *Yes, I can do this. I let him go once before, I can do it again.* But not a day would pass and I was desperately checking my email, waiting for a message from him. When there wasn't one, I felt frantic. Had he forgotten me? Had he decided it was over and staying away was the easier option than telling me? I would work myself into a frenzy and would become so angry, I would write to him that it was over. He would write back that he had been busy, it was hard for him to check his email all the time, that he couldn't bear to be away from me. And then we'd meet, kiss, hold hands and I would be happy once more, satisfied in his love.

We wanted more. I wanted more. I wanted to feel him be to me as intimate as a couple could be, but as it turned out, the situation, our meetings in a car, didn't allow for the type of love we wanted to make. So we sufficed by touching, holding, kissing. Oh, the kissing. He made me melt, the way he kissed me, with recklessness, with such hunger.

And once I was away from him, everything, the guilt, the hate for myself, the resentment towards him, came flooding back and I knew it had to end.

Once I began an argument about Shelby, an incident that I knew he was so sorrowful about. Another time, I accused him of not caring for me enough, for using me when we were kids. And there was one time where I told him this was it. "Done," I wrote one morning and waited for a reply. "I understand," he wrote back. A feeling of relief began to envelop me and I felt strong, knowing I had those moments where I could be away from him, that if I busied myself, I could do it. But by the evening I was a nervous wreck, checking my emails, hoping for a message from him, angry that he didn't fight me on it this time.

"I'm struggling," I wrote.

A message popped up almost immediately. "I know. I'm sitting here, staring at my phone. I don't know how to deal with this."

"Tell me how to deal with this," I begged.

"We can back off a bit," he wrote. "We can still talk, maybe just … I don't know. But I can't give you up."

"I can't either," I replied.

"Goodnight, my love," he wrote.

"Goodnight, baby," I replied.

I went to bed that night relieved that he still loved me, that he found it just as hard to let go. I wondered how it was going to end, as it eventually had to. But I knew that I couldn't leave him, didn't yet have the strength to. I had been thinking about it more and more, working out ways in which we could still keep in touch as just friends. Now, the idea of breaking contact obsessed me. How to do it, how to get over it. How was it that I was able to let him go as an obsessed teenager, but now, a mature adult, knowing the risk I was putting my family in, the man whom I loved more than anything, yes, even more than him, how could I not let him go now? I had to try again and somehow he knew by the coolness via email that it was coming.

He waited for me in his car and I got in, my heart beating hard, a lump in my throat. The look on his face showed me he understood my intention. I leaned back, away from him and he kept his distance. I lowered my gaze. There were a few moments of silence, where I noticed his fingers twitched and I kept my hands firmly tucked in my lap.

"So," I began and peered up at his face, which was staring at mine with an intensity, a fear.

I lost it then; I leapt off the seat and kissed him, long and hard, holding the tears that were threatening to fall down my face. I felt his warm mouth on mine, his hands reach out to mine and I squeezed them. I couldn't do it. I couldn't let him go. We were both as trapped as each other. I knew I had opened a can of worms that couldn't crawl back from where they came.

Did I hate myself? Of course. I would be an animal if I didn't. I felt like an animal, giving in to my urges, loving a man who I shouldn't. My betrayal was worse than anything Freddie could have ever done to me. I was living a double life, unable to end it with the man whom I had loved as a kid, the one who had hurt me, the one who got away, yet still in love with the man who saved me from him, the man who gave me his heart and soul, my life, my children.

So … where did it end?

It was a slow process. A tough slog. Trying to keep away from him, Freddie, for his part, trying to do the same. It took another four months before we stopped seeing each other altogether. The messages continued for a while beyond that, messages of desperation, of sadness, knowing we were never going to be together. There was no light at the end of the tunnel we had travelled.

It's been four years now and it's been a long and painful process, trying to rid Freddie from my head. I'm succeeding slowly but it took a while before I could accept that he never really did belong back in my life, nor I in his. My life belonged with the man I had married, the man whom I could never tell about what I'd done. Oh, I wanted to. So many times I wanted to spill it all to him; in fact, at one point, I thought it would have to take my confession to end this. My love for my husband, his pain, would make me forget, give me the ability to stay away for I know he really is the most important part of my life. But I know how selfish that is, to hurt him for what I had done. I had been selfish enough. It may be a cop-out but my continuing guilt is my penance, something I will live with forever.

It's better now. Sometimes days, even weeks go by when I don't yearn for Freddie. But he is always in the back of my mind. In a song, in a scene of a movie. I've accepted that he will be a part of my life, at least in my heart. I will let him go, in time. As I did before. And maybe this time it will be closure.

I knew it was a choice to love him again and it is a choice to unlove him. I'm working on it.

Kipp and Grace - *Words of Love* *

We were five or six when we met; it would be nice to say it was love at first sight but the truth is quite the opposite. I was so painfully shy as a kid, barely looking at or speaking to her at first, she was so beautiful. The way her cobalt blue eyes glimmered and that long black hair that just shone; I get butterflies just thinking about her even now.

For reasons then unknown, Grace took a liking to me; it seemed that she would go out of her way to talk to me, spend time with me. We even started walking to and from school together. Because she lived close we became inseparable and before I even knew what love actually was, it was reality; you know, the kind of love that I'd see her face when I closed my eyes — it was love, a deep, comfortable kind of love.

Telling her about these feelings was beyond me; other guys seemed to do it so naturally which made me a bit envious of their confident natures, of how easily they could approach a girl, but the fear of rejection and ridicule was just too much for me back then.

So just before the end of Year Nine, I wrote her a story, my first one, and with all the courage I could muster, slipped it into her book bag. I still remember the words like it was yesterday.

"*If I said*

You're beautiful, would my heart be revealed

Would you want me to keep these feelings concealed

Times spent with you, a new world comes into view

Star-crossed love it would be if you felt it too

Could it be something that we aren't meant to miss

Perhaps our souls have always been destined to kiss

…

If I said

I love you, would it change what or who we are

Will these three words spoken aloud go a step too far

Friends that's what we've always been

One another to which we've never seen

Learning about each other has captured my heart

Is it foolish to say? Where do I start

If I said

All that nourishes has been living in your time

Could this love be of a different kind

More than what just the physical could ever mean

It's chemical, spiritual, it's beautiful yet remained unseen

If I said

These things I want to say

Would it throw our lives in disarray

I wonder if you would just smile and take my hand

Under starlight together would we start to understand

Quiet conversations whispering into the night

Tender moments like in this story I write

If I said ..."

I didn't notice that she had found the note before the end of the day, but on the way home she stopped walking and looked at me with the note in her outstretched hand.

"Did you write this?" she asked in a stern voice.

I was speechless, must have gone pale, probably mouth wide open; I'd never heard that tone in her voice before. "I thought we were friends!" she muttered as she stormed past me.

Me being totally shocked, not able to talk as my mouth had gone instantly dry, and feeling my eyes glassing over, all I could do was watch her walk away. Suddenly she stopped, turned around and walked towards me. She grabbed my wrist, the note still clutched in her other hand, and she practically dragged me the rest of the way home. At her door, she looked at me, defiantly with angry eyes and clenched teeth, which meant she was serious. "Write me another note," she said, then slammed the door in my face.

It took me an entire sleepless night to write her a second note. Grace was the most beautiful girl in the school and in my world, I was a chubby shy guy and how naïve was I to think that I had a chance to be her person?

Resigning myself to the fact that I had ruined our friendship by saying that I loved her left me with nothing to lose, so holding nothing back I poured my heart out in that note.

The next day she didn't meet me as usual, so off I went to school, alone for the first time in a while, wondering if it had been a waste of time, almost making me hope she would just leave it all alone.

When our eyes met that morning, all I got was an expressionless stare. I was feeling heartbroken but still determined to let her know how my feelings, even though it was already out there and nothing was going to put this genie back in that bottle. Nervously I slipped the note into her bag, as we silently passed in class, before sitting far away from her at the front.

So flustered, knowing what I had written, she was probably reading it before we sat down, hoping the sweat rolling down my face wasn't also dripping down my back and showing on my shirt. Each word was seared in my mind; I began to recite it, hoping she was reading in time with me.

"Love doesn't struggle for the light

It's growth from the seeds of friendship

Cultivated nurtured with patience

Supported by the heartstrings of care

Enchanting the sun to shine

Inspiring the stars to fill the night's sky

A song that only two hearts can sing

Starting as a quiet melody first

Perhaps very hard to hear

Rhythms existing in the beating of hearts

Over time the harmonies become clear

This song is written by a daydream

Experience holds us back

Yet forward we step

It's the fear, the hope and the passion

Faith that love isn't a fleeting thing

The measure of true love's kindness

Learning that vulnerability is strength

Respect is the truth of understanding

Trust is love's greatest gift

Is it naive to dream this way?

Does love's adventure begin like this?

A look, a word, a touch

When two souls caress unseen

Is it the tender moments of discovery?

Realizing that love exists here

Soulmates come to life, to light

Have they always been there?

Waiting for this song to begin?

Love isn't contingent on reciprocation

Nor is it a quest for validation

Love is the true desire to see happiness

Hopefully to feel the happiness too

Imagine what I said was to you ..."

I could feel her staring at me but I refused to look back at her for fear of what I may see.

"Oh my," said a voice from behind me and there was no mistaking that it came from Grace. Within moments she was standing in front of me and I could see the rest of the class had gone silent. All eyes must have been on us.

"You wrote this?" she asked in that stern voice of hers, her hands on her waist. I was not even able to nod in my shocked state.

She leaned down and kissed me on the lips.

"I love you too!" she said, and sat beside me.

Summer love, glorious, crazy, beautiful: we were inseparable since that wonderful day.

Now, she's gone, her father transferred to another country; suddenly it was like it never happened. We stayed in touch for a bit in letters, the odd phone call, but distance doesn't favour young love.

Grace never left my thoughts or heart for these forty years, the words and feelings are just as vibrant and real as they were then … but there are still things that I need to say but can't; the note is ready, I just need to know where to send it. Only then will she know I never stopped loving and thinking about her. In my nostalgic reminiscence wondering if she thinks of me too. If we found each other again I would put the note in her hand.

"Apart we have been for many years

Your leaving filled my soul with tears

I held hope that you were not really lost

To share these words with you at any cost

Hope that in this life we will be reunited

Fires that long ago were ignited

This love I feel has no limit

My heart's soul has been counting every minute

Feelings written as a tender embrace

A love that not even time can't erase

Will my note find you? it's up to fate

Because you are my soulmate ..."

From time to time over the years I've tried to find her with no success; just to reconnect and to know if happiness has been a part of her life would be enough ...

*This story was authored by Kipp Roane.

Jeffrey and Catrina - *A Love That Hurts*

September 1, 2015

I met the love of my life today. He is the one I know will be forever. How do I know this? You just know, right? And it's the right time in my life, I know it. Okay, so he's tall, like over six foot, like a basketball player. I like that he's tall. I can imagine raising myself on one foot to kiss him. He has sandy brown hair and looks skinny, lanky, and he wears glasses, which I think is kind of sexy. He has this shy look about him and my gosh, it's such a difference from those other macho hotshots with their oiled-up beefy bodies, trying to sell themselves as players. I'm over players. I've had players and none of them live up to the hype. All a bunch of letdowns. Big talkers with average everythings. But not this one. Jeffrey, by the way; that's his name.

And I'm going to swipe right!

September 2, 2015

I'm meeting him tomorrow! He lives right next to uni, in the off-campus housing. Convenient! So excited, I need to figure out what to wear. Go casual? But maybe a little make-up … just to highlight my eyes. They are my best assets. I don't want him to be looking at my other assets and if he does, well, then I don't know. I've had guys that are only interested in one thing. I'm so over that. I've been partying since I finished high school, two years ago, and I'm over it. I'm ready to settle. Okay, enough with that. Now gotta find something to wear. Yay!

September 5, 2015

Best date ever!!!

Okay, so I'll start from the beginning. Firstly, after a lot of changing of clothes, I finally settled for jeans and a red top. I look good in red, I know – it highlights my skin, which my mum calls porcelain, and also it goes with my dark hair, which I straightened. I didn't wear any make-up except for mascara. I wanted to keep it casual, like I wasn't trying too hard. But then before I left, I almost cancelled I was so nervous and I kept changing my mind about whether he was the right one at all. But what do I have to lose, yeah?

When I saw him, after my class, I knew it was the right thing to do, to meet this guy. He smiled, so cool, so warm, and pulled me in for a hug. Now I'm a talker, but I felt a bit awkward and couldn't think of anything to say. We made small talk, you know, what are you studying – he was studying dentistry, by the way, weird, but who am I to judge – I had no clue what I was going to do with my life, studying a general arts degree in the hope of figuring it out by the time the course is complete ... anyway, we talked awkwardly all the way up to his room on the seventh floor. I know, what was I doing, going to some guy's room when I have just met him? I don't know. I just did. But I liked his voice. He was soft-spoken, clearly enunciated his words, had this way about him like he was smart, like he knew things, that he was worldly.

He sat in a desk chair and I sat on the edge of his bed. I could see he was a bit nervous so I thought I might try to ease the awkwardness. I took off my shoes and folded my feet under my legs. And then when I looked up, he was pulling what looked like a bong towards him, from under the study table! "You don't mind?" he says to me and I'm just shaking my head, trying not to show that I'm freaking out. I've never seen a bong before and I watched in confusion.

Is this a red flag? I didn't really know what to do but he chatted a little as he smoked this thing and I nodded and acknowledged his words as I stared at what he was doing in fascination. The next thing I know he's next to me, leaning on the bed head. He put his hand on my leg and it felt weird, so awkward, like he wasn't sure what to do, so I leaned over and kissed him. And that's when I knew. This is it. I know, I know, too soon, but yeah, we did it. And then it was brilliant. We made coffee, listened to music, sang songs together, I even rapped a song about him, and he loved it. I didn't want the night to end.

September 10, 2015

It's been a few days, but more to come. I just didn't want to forget about this morning so I need to put it down. He got me this massive bunch of flowers and this beautiful note. "For the most beautiful girl in the world. I want to be yours." But it's not official yet.

September 21, 2015

It's official. We're on.

Lots to catch you up on. I've just had zero time.

Firstly, a bit about Jeffrey. His friends call him Jeff but I prefer to call him Jeffrey, his full name, which sounds so much better. His fam is wealthy, but he has some baggage. His sister died right in front of him, on a sailboat. She was epileptic and had a seizure in the water when they were swimming. I think he blames himself because his parents were in the cabin and he feels like he didn't get to her quick enough, like he could have done more, but what more could be have done, right? He was only six at the time and she was five. I mean, his parents should maybe have been keeping a better eye on them.

Speaking of. I met them yesterday, not entirely sure how I feel about them. He seems nice, tall, made me feel welcome, but his mother, I don't know, kind of treated me like I was beneath them, like he was too good for me or something. I mean, she was nice, but I felt like she was a bit fake … don't know how to explain.

So maybe he is a bit damaged, which is fine because I think I can be there for him. It's nice he can talk to me about these things and I can help him sort through how he feels when he needs to … I hope anyway.

I like him a lot; I mean, a lot. He is kind, caring, always asking if I'm okay. He reminds me of my little bro, not so little but soft-hearted, gentle, thoughtful. I think I want to keep this one.

September 29, 2015

Just touching base. Everything is so good. We are so aligned, like this was meant to be the whole time. I think we met at the right time in our lives. We are so compatible and I just want to spend every minute with him. Kayla is irritated with me because I had to cancel on our girls' night out, but Jeffrey wanted to take me out that night, so I mean, she has to understand, right? I don't think he likes Kayla though, but I will have to make them see eye to eye and if they care about me they need to. I'm trying to set up a date for Kayla and another friend, Jess, to meet with us for lunch or even drinks.

Oh and I swear, when he touches me, I want to faint! And yeah, he told me he loved me. I never wanted anyone to say it so much and when he did, wow!

October 29, 2015

It's been a long few weeks. I just read my last notes and no, the meeting didn't happen. He didn't want to meet them and to be honest, I was a little pissed with them because they really weren't making the effort either. So bugger them. My mum told me that's usually what happens, and the good friends stick around. I haven't spoken to Kayla in a week and we used to be on the phone all the time.

Jeffrey. So I don't quite know what to say. I love him. He's told me he loves me too, he says it all the time. It's going well, I guess, but when I talked about his baggage before, I didn't realised how much he has packed (haha, pun there). I'm there for him when he talks about his stuff though, mainly his sister, but sometimes I feel like he puts a lot on me too.

I mean, does he need to keep bringing up things from my past? Like the other day, he was talking about Alan. I only mentioned Alan to him because Alan was my last boyfriend who honestly didn't even last a month but because I slept with Alan he has an issue with him. He told me I had to delete Alan from my socials, which I guess makes sense so I did, but he keeps bringing it up. And he asks me about other guys on my socials. Most of them are only friends but he is jealous. At first I was flattered; he's jealous and if he's jealous it's a good thing, right? But it's getting tiring. I don't know how to tell him that he's the only one I want. All the others in my past don't matter. And those people on my socials, well, I deleted a few in front of him and I guess they are not that important anyway. I mean, he is now my life, I suppose.

December 1, 2015

Holidays are here so I have more time on my hands. Today I put up the Christmas tree with my mum. It's a tradition we have every year. We play Christmas songs loudly and sing and all of us put up the tree and decorate the house. I wasn't so into it this year and my sister noticed. I think Mum noticed too but she didn't say anything, she just tried to make me sing so I would get into the mood.

But Jeffrey was a bit pissed because it was the only time he had to go shopping and he guilted me. He said he was my priority now and I should put him first. So I hurried the work and took off. He still wasn't happy when we met up though. We just walked around the shopping centre and he left early. I was a bit sad about the whole thing. I mean, should I be putting him first? I think maybe I should, since he is my future, but surely he could understand that I had something important to do, but he didn't think it was important. But when his dad calls him to help out at their business, he runs off and I'm expected to understand. I don't know.

January 8, 2016

I think we're done. I love him but I don't know how much more I can take of it. I don't even know where to start, there's so much. I don't even know who to talk to anymore. I can't talk to Mum because she will freak out, I don't even have Kayla anymore. I can talk to April but my sister is busy, she has a life of her own and honestly, I'm probably making excuses because I don't want anyone to judge him.

He has issues, I said that from day one, but no one will understand that. They will just see how I am. It's weird but you don't see yourself changing and suddenly you're there, this person that wasn't this person before and if it's a better person then that's fine, but I don't think I'm a better person. I feel like I've withdrawn from people. I lie and smile and tell everyone that everything is fine but it's not. I don't know how to make things okay anymore. Nothing I say is good enough or makes him happy anymore. But when I tell him that we need to have some space maybe, because we're arguing so much, he says awful things. The other day he said he has no life without me and he will end it all if I leave him. I know he didn't mean it but it's shit to feel like responsible for someone even if it also felt a little good that I was there for him. I do love him though.

January 16, 2016

I'm sitting in my room by myself. The parents are out and Keith and April are not home either. It's the first time I've been by myself for a while. It's nice but it's also a bit unnerving. Being alone with my thoughts — well. I don't know if I want to be with Jeffrey anymore. But I also don't know if anyone on this planet will love me like he does. I mean, I see crazy in his love but crazy is good, right? He is mad jealous about anyone, to the point where he calls me a whore for having a history that hadn't included him. I know I shouldn't let him but I can see such emotion in him, I try to pacify him because he is so on the edge sometimes.

I know at the beginning I didn't want him to do drugs but now I almost make him, just to calm him. Sometimes I need it myself. No, I don't take the hard stuff, just a bong or a smoke every now and then. Just to keep him company usually but I don't know... When I'm out with him and his friends and the only one not doing anything... it's a bit weird. I guess I shouldn't do things to fit in — I never really have, but ...

Maybe I'm giving up too easily. I feel guilty just thinking like this about him because really, I do love him. And he has got some really good things. I mean, we go up to his parents' holiday house every couple of weeks and it's really nice there, no one but us. We swim in the pool and play on the beach. We snuggle next to each other all night and he whispers beautiful things in my ear. How I'm the most beautiful girl he's seen, how we are going to be together forever. Even after he has hurt me, he doesn't know he's hurt me but he holds me and I feel comfort.

March 2, 2016

Just had my birthday party — 21. Supposed to be so good, a big celebration at home. My parents let me have it at home. But it was the worst night. Kayla came to the party and Jeffrey was not happy. They said something to each other and Kayla took off. So I asked him about it and he called me a whore again. I tried to let him be so I could take care of my guests but he just sat in my room and yelled at me every time I walked in. I tried to calm him down, even my mum told him to get a grip, that this was a celebration, and eventually he came out but I just couldn't wait for the night to be over.

I think I need to have some space from him. I need to figure out what I want from him. I'm unhappy, I can see that now, but I don't know what I can do about it.

April 29, 2016

I'm exhausted. It's all arguments and all making love. It sounds like some cheesy book or some cheesy movie. He loves me but he also hates me sometimes. I know I feed off his jealousy but sometimes I think he is jealous of more than my past. When I talk about finishing university and specialising in teaching or media, he puts me down, makes me feel like I can't do it, when I know I can. Is that because he is insecure? I finally talked to April about things. She's tough though. She says I should get the hell out of this toxic relationship, but I can't, not yet. He needs me and in all honesty, I need him. It's not so much that he makes me happy like he used to, but it's like I just need him, like he belongs in my life ... I don't know how to explain it but I can't *not* be in his life.

The violence frightens me sometimes, even though I consider myself a tough bitch. I can look him right in the eye when he's got my hands above my head, my back against the wall; I mean, literally—I had bruises around my wrists the last time and I covered them with bracelets. Yesterday he leaned so close to me when he yelled, there was saliva all over my face and when I tried to leave after he pushed me on the bed, he got on the floor in front of me and grabbed my knees together and cried into them. He said he would kill himself if I left, so what was I supposed to do? I stayed. But I couldn't sleep. I need to think about what to do next. I miss him already and it's only been a couple of hours since I've seen him. I can't even remember what the argument was about.

Funny, I can never remember what the arguments are about. It's never anything serious enough to warrant an argument.

June 12, 2016

It's been a while, hey? Life is, well, it's life, haha. No, probably not that funny. I think we broke up. But I don't know. Last night was crazy, crazier than the other times when he sometimes locks me out of his apartment after dragging me out there, leaving me alone, and crazier when he opened the car door and pushed me out in the middle of the freeway.

No, last night was bad. We were at his parents' holiday home in Bright and it was a stupid argument. It's always a stupid argument, but this time it was about how to pronounce the word mischievous. He got pretty shitty when he googled it and I was right and he screamed at me, calling me a know-it-all and put his fist to my face. So I packed my stuff and tried to leave, knowing I was having a panic attack, which has been happening more often lately. By the time I had my stuff ready, he had locked all the doors with a key and hid the key so I locked myself in a room and called April.

He could hear I was on the phone and screamed and threatened to kill me so I hung up and came out, but then he just lunged at me and picked me right up off the floor. His eyes were black and crazy and he pushed me to the railing of the staircase and leaned me over the stairwell. We were one storey up. "Your life is in my hands." He said that clearly. "I could kill you right now if I wanted to. Do you want to die?" I don't think I will forget those words.

I cried and begged and he pulled me forward and threw me to the floor at his feet. My legs were thumping in pain and I could only think about the fact that there would be some nice bruises on them tomorrow and what I was going to wear that could cover them and it's okay, it's winter, so it should be fine.

I went to the bedroom and he came with me and put me on the bed next to him and wrapped his arms around me. I don't know if he fell asleep, but I didn't. I was awake all night and I forgave him; I don't know why but I forgave him for the night before. I don't know where we stand right now because I left before he got out of the shower.

June 30, 2016

Things are good. I think we needed to have that big fight to make us realise that we really love each other. He's been so good. Really caring, bought me flowers and sent a big teddy bear to my house. We haven't really talked about the incident but I know he's sorry. I feel bad for how sorry he must be. It's also good because we are having a bit of space. Space as in we don't see each other every single day. Every second day sometimes and last week we made it to three! We talk on the phone every day though. I think we may be getting on track. Maybe it was just too much at once, too much expectation as well. I mean, I went into this believing he may be the one. Those expectations are way too high for someone to live up to.

July 16, 2016

And we broke up. He doesn't love me apparently. How could he not love me?! After everything he's put me through, after all the crap he's dealt and I've taken. What the fuck!

I'm feeling really down. Well, at least he gave me some ideas on where to get the stuff from, so it helps. It sucks to do it alone but it takes the edge off. I don't know if I've faced it yet? It hasn't hit me, I don't think ... maybe it's not over? I don't know but I still talk to him. We at least text each other every day. I mean, if he doesn't love me like he said why would he be wasting his time on me? I know I miss him already though.

August 18, 2016

So we're back on. I knew it! I knew he still loved me!

August 29, 2016

I have my suspicions. I think he may be cheating. How do you ask someone if they are cheating? Sounds stupid! But that's not the problem right now. I just had to do the most embarrassing thing. Go to the doctor for a STD test! Chlamydia! Yes, he was with someone for that little time we were apart. Not that we were really apart. I mean, we were still sort of seeing each other! But I didn't know he was sleeping with someone else. I can't really be upset, can I, because we weren't together. But shit, can I at least be upset that he just passed on some fricken disease to me!

September 15, 2016

It's been a year. But we have broken up. Maybe for good this time. But we keep finding each other. I guess I don't give up easily. I want to see how it goes, give him a chance. I know he can be a good person. But even though we're not together, we still have each other and it's good because it's not such a shock to completely be away from one another. We were good for a while before that but the drugs are too much. He has these nightmares and his moods are crazy. I know I wanted to be the one to help him through this, but I know I can't be, he needs more help than I can give him. It's hard to sit and watch this happen to him but it's harder to leave him to deal with it all by himself. He needs me and I need him and until we can get over this, whatever it is, we will still be there for each other. Maybe it can turn into friendship? Haha, no, that's not going to happen. But this weird relationship seems to be working. We're not fighting so much anymore.

He's calling me right now.

September 29, 2016

My chest hurts so much right now. I don't know what to think.

I found a girl's underpants tucked between his bed and his window when I went over to surprise him. It was late, around one a.m., and he was asleep so I cuddled beside him and he put his arm around me. That's when I felt it. He said it was a friend who lived next door and used the shower because her hot water wasn't working. I want to believe him but I'm not stupid. But he sat there and begged me to believe him, told me there was no one but me.

I mean, if he wanted someone else, why does he want me, right? He said he never loved anyone like he loved me, that I was his world. I mean, we were giving it another go, exclusively this time. So I want to believe him, that he loves me and that he wouldn't do anything to jeopardise what we have. I confided to April and to my mum. They both think it's bullshit but they also know that I do what I want to do, that they can't convince me not to believe him. I look so stupid to everyone. You know, if someone told me that about themselves, I would tell them to leave the fucker and don't look back. But I think I want to believe him. I'm not ready yet to let go.

September 30, 2016

We're done. I've spent another sleepless night and I can't get it out of my head. I've broken it off. I've deleted him from everything. It's over.

October 8, 2016

We've been messaging again. He's sorry, still hasn't admitted to anything but he's so sorry and I feel so sorry for him. But I need to stick to my guns. I can be there for him when he gets in his moods when he's feeling like shit. I think I'll always be there for him and he said he needs me in his life. But I'm doing okay. I'm having fun again, seeing my friends again, even Kayla has come around a couple of times and I'm getting back to who I used to be. Fun, free, happy, not constantly tormented by this relationship.

November 4, 2016

I don't know what I'm doing anymore. I am back with Jeffrey but I don't know why. I guess I still love him. We were doing okay as friends and then somehow he realised he couldn't live without me. Actually said he would kill himself if I wasn't in his life. I told him I still was in his life but he was making plans for our future together which sounded nice. I've agreed and hopefully it can work out somehow. I mean, clearly we still need each other, on my part too. And I care about him. I know we can work this out.

December 27, 2016

He's away. With his family in Egypt. His father is Egyptian, did I mention that? Yeah, so they go there every couple of years. For four weeks he's gone. But he promised that when he gets back we are going to move in together, so that's something to look forward to, I suppose.

December 31, 2016

It's New Year's Eve and I miss him. It's lonely knowing he is on the other side of the world.

January 26, 2017

So his family have returned but he's still in Egypt. He says it's to housesit a family friend's house while they are on holiday. But honestly, something doesn't feel right. I'm trying not to look too deep into it and to be honest, it's been quite nice being on my own here. Even though we are together, I've been out with my friends again, having fun, returning to normal. I've been spending more time with my family, actually enjoyed being with them, being normal, not having to watch my words in case they were used against me. People accept me and that's hard to understand. It never used to be. I think things need to change when he gets back, I need to become who I was before him because isn't that the person he liked, that he was attracted to? Now I don't even know who I am without him. But it's nice finding out, finding myself. Especially since it's so hard to even be in touch with him. Yeah, there's always the time difference thing but he's seriously hard to catch.

I'm more confused than ever. I want him to come back but in the pit of my stomach I feel … I don't know, resentment? That he separated me from everything that I love that I was starting to become close to again, my family, my friends. I don't know when he is coming home; he said in a couple of weeks but I don't know how to feel about it. I don't know whether I want him to.

February 18, 2017

He came back, I picked him up from the airport myself. I almost believed he was genuinely excited to see me, but he was a master manipulator after all. He could make me believe anything he wanted to. We slept together last night, for what would be the last time, and I woke up this morning without him in bed next to me and the pit in my stomach grew instantly.

I knew what I had to do. I picked up my phone and went into his Instagram followers, and there were four new women he was following. One of them stood out to me and I went into her profile and there it was, a post about how glad she was to meet him as they cuddled closely in the photo.

He walked into the room, and lied. "It was my parents' friend." I said it wasn't and I explained what I had found.

He lied again. "I didn't sleep with her."

But I knew enough by the way he wouldn't lock his eyes with mine. He was too tired of the lies to even try anymore. I broke down and cried and asked God why over and over, before I finally stood up, thanked him for ruining my life, and told him I never wanted to ever see him again.

September 21, 2017

A Facebook memory popped up today. Two years ago. 'It's official' and   there's a photo of Jeffrey and me at a restaurant. He's got his arms around me and   I'm looking into his eyes while I take the photograph.

A knot starts to turn in my stomach. No, not a knot of yearning, a knot of disgust. That I gave so much of myself to this guy. I didn't look back. I deleted him from everything and tried not to think about him again. Of course that's hard but those thoughts were regret. You know how people say you will be better for those experiences, the ones that change you; I don't know if that's the case here.

But when I looked at that picture I also realised I was a long way from that girl who let herself be manipulated, let herself be hit, let herself be abused by a man who didn't know her worth. He had no self-worth himself, I see that now, and I tried to change that, for so long. But I know now I couldn't change it, I was delusional to think I had that power. I feel sorry for him because unless something drastic happens or he finds a reason to become a better person, he will wallow in the muck he's created around himself; he will always thrive on the pity that people give him.

I thought he was my forever guy, even through the tough stuff. I know better now. I used to imagine him lying dead on the side of the road or someone calling to tell me he'd killed himself. Yes, I still worried but I knew my own limits too. I was of no help to him as much as my hubris believed I could help him.

He tried to reach out to me once, asking if I could meet him to give back his jumper.

I mailed it to his apartment.

Derek and Daisy- *Enough*

I don't condone cheating. Never. But until you've been in my shoes, don't judge.

That sounds harsh, I know, but maybe that's my way of forgiving myself. Not just for cheating, but for staying in a relationship out of pity. Her name was Paula. No, she's not my Billy, but a bit of background would help to understand where I stood.

Paula was the older woman, worldly, the wife of Robbie, the marriage at which I was the MC. I was with Cherie, my high school sweetheart, and we befriended the couple. From the outset I could see that it was a strained marriage and less than a year later, it was all but over.

So was my relationship with Cherie, and Paula and I kept in touch. I was a mere twenty-year-old and to be so needed by this charming woman sent me into a head spin. I thought I was in love, had found the woman of my dreams, but Paula was my mentor, taught me about life, about sex, about society. She took me into her world and I moved in with her almost immediately once we made our relationship official. Even then, I had doubts, as much as I was enjoying everything this woman provided; in short, I was enamoured, by her lifestyle, her maturity, her place in society as an assistant fashion director at a large firm.

Four years later, after I had begun working as a drama teacher as well as directing in the local playhouse in a little country town, Paula and I tied the knot. It just seemed the necessary next step, but the marriage began to deteriorate almost immediately and I knew we had made a mistake. Within the year, we had already begun discussing separation. It was just about this time when Paula's father was diagnosed with leukaemia and as the hospital was conveniently close to our flat, her parents stayed with us frequently. As we didn't want to add stress to her parents, we pretended our marriage was strong and agreed to fake it until we made it or until the inevitable happened. I was quite happy to accommodate; after all, I may not have been in love with Paula, but I did love her. She was a kind, caring woman, who turned me into a man.

I just didn't expect to meet the woman who I thought I would love forever. Her name was Daisy and when she auditioned for a part in a new play at the playhouse where I worked in the evenings, I was mesmerised.

"Who is that?" I nudged John, the director/owner of the playhouse.

"How am I supposed to know, mate, but she's cute." He laughed crudely.

For some reason that made me irritated, like he was degrading someone I knew. "Have a little respect," I muttered and put my focus back on this woman. I had to know who she was, this elfin beauty, who looked so innocent, so young. And then she smiled, not directly at me, but that smile was for me and I felt like my heart stopped. I swallowed hard, not comprehending this feeling. And she was good, really good, not just her effervescent beauty, but her acting chops. Of course, she got the part but for some reason I was scared to talk to her and I let John do the talking while I, usually an extrovert, slunk behind, my tongue quite tied.

I went home that night feeling an acute sense of sadness, for the life I should have had. I was twenty-five years old, I should not have been in a long-term relationship, a loveless one at that. And despite myself, I was looking forward to the beginning of rehearsals.

Now, as I said, I'm not a shy guy and usually I go for what I want, but this woman had put me off-kilter and I found it hard to begin a conversation with her, even though she would flash me that killer smile every time our eyes met. I would usually throw back a lopsided one and scurry away. What was it about this woman with legs that stretched to heaven and a smile that thrust me into hell? It was obsessive the way I thought about her and when she was on that stage, I was a goner; I could feel my heart warming, a glow of pride surrounding it, especially when she poured out the emotion, particularly in one scene in which her evil, abusive father put a shotgun to the back of her head while threatening her on-stage mother, before raising it above her head and firing it into the air. I remember always holding my breath during that scene in particular, in awe of the emotion that Daisy exuded.

"Hey, Derek, how did I go?" she said one day as she walked past me, heading off stage, and I just nodded.

At the end of the evening, as I was leaving the playhouse, I found Daisy sitting on the front steps and I hesitated. "Waiting for a lift?" She nodded and I looked around. Not many people were about and I sat beside her.

"Who's picking you up?" I asked.

"My sister. I don't live very far but it's a bit late. So I don't really want to walk home by myself." She looked at me. "You don't have to wait here for me," she said. "I'm a big girl."

I was curious about her age. It was hard to gauge. She seemed mature but looked like a girl with those massive eyes that seemed to stare into nowhere. "Yeah, one that doesn't want to walk home alone." I said with a laugh. "It's okay, I don't live too far away either. Hey, do you want a lift?"

"Cath's already on her way."

I felt a stab of disappointment. That meant that her sister would be here any minute. "So what do you do other than act in your spare time?"

"I'm studying to be a teacher," she said. "I have a year to go." I knew that already. It was in her portfolio. Her age wasn't in there!

"Well, I'm a teacher, down at the Catholic school."

"Oh yeah?" Her eyes lit up. "I think I may get a placement there next year. At least I'm hoping I do."

Again a buzz of excitement went through me. "It's a good school. What are you specialising in?"

At that moment, a car drove into the carpark and Daisy looked towards it and when she looked back at me, I thought I sensed the disappointment I was feeling, reflected in her eyes. "See you on Thursday?"

"Yeah," I said and got to my feet. I watched as she skipped to the car and as she opened the door, she turned around and gave me a wave, flashing that smile.

I kept that image with me for the next few days, letting it brighten my day when things became too strained at home.

It became a routine, one I looked forward to more than the show itself. The few minutes after the rehearsal when everyone was leaving and I waited with Daisy for her sister to pick her up. I learned about her life, little things, like her favourite pastime, charcoal drawings, and one night she brought some to show me, beautiful intricately drawn people doing everyday things: reading on a street bench, a sleeping woman on a tram, a woman sitting at a bus stop, her hand on the handle of a baby carriage. I felt touched she wanted me to see something so personal and I was overwhelmed with affection when she pulled out one from the bottom of the pile of me, just a quick sketch of my facial features but so well drawn I knew it was me.

When the show opened, it was a busy time, the usual excitement and frenzy filling the theatre, but I was thinking about Daisy and how I couldn't fathom not having those few moments every rehearsal night with her.

The show went well, not as sold out as we'd hoped, but it was a good run and at the after party, Daisy and I spent some time sitting on the stairs, where we had a conversation so intimate, I never felt anything like I was feeling before. She, by now, knew I was married but now I confided to her about the state of my marriage. She listened quietly but when she looked at me with not pity but love, I knew I had never felt like this about Paula. Ever.

I went home that night hating myself for being in love with someone who was not my wife, but at night as I lay in bed with my wife turned to the other side, I thought about Daisy, the smooth skin on her hand which she usually waved about as she talked animatedly about something; I thought about her lips, not too full, and I imagined putting my own on them. I squeezed my eyes tight knowing how wrong this was to do, but feeling heavenly at the anticipation.

I knew, especially after tonight, that Paula was not the lasting love I thought she would be. The conversation I'd had with Daisy just hours before confirmed this, a connection, a chemistry that was there from the moment I talked to her. In all our time together, Paula had never made me feel half the things that Daisy touched in me this night. I felt an acute sense of sadness, not just for my situation, but for my wife. I had let her down by not feeling for her what I should have been. I would never love her as I should have.

The next evening before the show, Daisy found me in the hallway as she was heading to stage for the sound check. I smiled at her and she walked straight to me, held my arm and reached forward, kissing me on my mouth. A quick kiss but one that shook my soul. "For luck," she said and bolted away.

"Nice," said John, who was heading through the hallway.

"For luck," I said, trying to find my bearings, and when he'd walked past, I shook my head, trying to get my head into the show. Everything went to plan and she was even better than the night before. My eyes were glued to her and after the show, when the audience had dispersed, I waited for her on the steps. She came out and sat beside me. She looked sad.

"Are you okay?" I asked, worried that she regretted having kissed me.

"I'm sorry," she said. "You know, for the kiss thing."

"Are you really sorry?"

She looked up at me and shook her head slowly.

****

Then something happened. It was weird the timing, almost kismet. Paula, I found out, was seeing someone else. A friend of mine, Darren, who worked with Paula, found her in the arms of a colleague and he took me out to dinner to let me know about it. It didn't seem like she was even hiding it all that much; she was in the smoker's garden at work and was sitting out in the open on the lap of the man, her arms around his neck, his hands on her chest. She didn't see Darren, who slunk away before either of them could.

When Darren related this to me, I don't really know what I felt. It didn't hurt me, I didn't feel any sense of being betrayed. I realise it must have been a relief!

Because by now, I had kissed Daisy. That very night she first kissed me and when I knew she felt the same I knew I wanted her more than anything I had ever wanted. When she looked up at me and nodded, I stood up and took her hand. I led her under a tree in the carpark and I put my mouth on hers. It was the sweetest kiss and I knew that we were connected, it felt so right.

So when I found out about Paula, it was liberation. I know it sounds dreadful but it just gave me permission to be who I wanted to be with Daisy. And we met often, usually after work, where we'd play in the car; sometimes I would risk going to her place which was not far from my school, sometimes at the local park, where we would just stroll together even if we were unable to hold hands.

I couldn't tell anyone about Daisy. Our relationship had to be kept a secret. I worked in a Catholic school and if it got out, there would be hell to pay, quite literally, and I justified it by the fact that we hadn't gone all the way, which really was silly considering we had done all but the deed. And really only because there was no real opportunity to do so.

Then one night, when in Melbourne for a play, I met up with Daisy and we went back to my hotel together. I shouldn't have felt the way I did. I should have felt terrible. I vividly remember that night, the first time we saw each other naked and spent the night together. We held each other, our naked bodies melting into each other all night. There was something so passionate, so sensual, I wanted this feeling to be with me forever.

I told Paula about Daisy a week later. There were tears, there was shouting but I knew I had ammunition and I threw her own affair at her. She was gobsmacked and I felt like shit doing it, but I was hoping that would be the beginning of the end. It wasn't, not yet. I continued seeing Daisy, thought about her every waking moment and every sleeping one too, but Paula kept putting off the conversation when I tried to talk about us parting ways. She had ended things with her guy, she told me, on the day of our fifth anniversary, when she donned her wedding dress and pleaded with me to try again.

I loved Paula, but not like that, and it hurt me to refuse her advances but I was long gone in love with Daisy and we were already making plans to be together. I couldn't imagine life without her now and despite Paula's constant arguments with me at home, I stayed on because I knew she needed me to be there.

Perhaps that was a cop-out. I don't know why I stayed for those months, maybe it was fear of the unknown, a fear of changing my whole life, letting people down, people thinking badly of me. It was horrid at home and now I had taken to sleeping on the couch every night I was at home. But now that everything was out in the open, I spent more time in Melbourne, weekends with Daisy, who was a pleasure to wake up with, the smell of her ash-blonde hair tossed over my shoulder, making little gurgling sounds as she slept. Making love in the morning, sometimes in the middle of the night, sometimes during dinner! And the talking, oh, the wonderful conversations about the theatre, watching movies, sharing music, drinking wine on the balcony of the apartment that she'd moved into, as we watched the lights and sounds of the city.

The day before my twenty-sixth birthday, I was home and discussing with Paula my need to begin my life without her. "I want to keep trying," she said.

"We aren't trying," I replied, disheartened that she wasn't getting it, that I wanted out.

"You aren't trying," she said, tears already in her eyes.

"Because I don't want to," I said. I had to say it straight. There was no beating around the bush anymore.

Her face changed, turned into a snarl, and she turned her wedding ring around. Then with the force of the Almighty, she slapped me across my face. "I hate you," she said and stormed out of the room.

I put my hand to my face which was still stinging and when I looked at my hand, it was smeared with blood. Well, at least the wedding ring worked for something now, I thought bitterly.

But it was over. I left, got a house nearer to my school and moved in a couple of weeks later.

Fate is a terrible thing, isn't it?

A few weeks after I was free, Daisy got a job teaching in a small town, more than five hours away from mine and it was harder to see her as often as we had done. But we did communicate via phone and texts, which got fewer and farther between. In the space of a year, we had seen each other four times, when she visited her family in my hometown and when I finally ventured up to see her. Things were good for that weekend, but we both knew it was not going to work and as much as I loved her, there was nothing I could do.

As it happened, after that year, she told me she was seeing someone. Bradley, his name was, a teacher at the school where she worked and as broken as I was, I couldn't do anything about it. I felt for her, so far away from home, from her family, from me. What could I do?

Well, I began dating too. Casual dating but then I met Loretta after a year or so. Daisy and I kept in touch but we always kept it platonic. Just a casual greeting every now and then, sometimes just news of work and family, that sort of thing. And then came the call.

"I'm getting married," she blurted when I answered the phone.

"Congratulations," I replied, trying to sound excited. My heart was on the floor but I knew it was inevitable. She had mentioned Bradley a few times in conversation and even though I never asked for details, I could hear the excitement in her voice when she talked about him.

"I don't know, Derek," she said uncertainly.

"Doubts?" I asked, not sure if that made me happy.

"No, no," she said quickly. "I mean, I love him …" My heart felt a stab but I swallowed so I could hear her out. "But we're … we're different."

"How?" I knew already. Daisy had explained Bradley. He may be rippling with muscles but he was devoid of culture. Not that it was necessarily a bad thing but I knew it was something Daisy loved about me. Being able to talk about art, theatre, books … Bradley's idea of a night out was going out for a pub meal on a Friday night and getting home early so he could awake early for footy training the next morning. And on most Saturday evenings, he would be out drowning his sorrows at the pub if he lost or celebrating at the same place if he won. That's when Daisy and I usually chatted, when she was alone at home waiting for her beau to get home. I hated hating him but I knew he would never make her happy. Not like I would.

"I mean … never mind." She paused. "Hey, Derek?"

"Yes?"

"Wish me the best?"

"I wish you all the best, Daisy, all the love in the world. You deserve it."

I looked at the phone after she'd hung up for the longest time and finally breathed. I vowed to be her friend and I wasn't going to hurt her by being upset about it. It sounds odd and I was jealous as fuck, but I knew that to keep her in my life, somehow even as a friend, I had to accept whatever she did. We had no choice in not being together anyway. Besides, how could I resent her for falling in love when I knew at the time, I was falling in love too.

Her name was Karen. Karen was a friend of a friend and when I met her at a party, we clicked right away. She was attractive, outgoing, knowledgeable and feisty. I felt that I needed Karen in my life but no, Karen was not a replacement for Daisy. I fell in love with Karen the more I got to know her and we had so much in common. She was open, so much so, I had no qualms in sharing my history with Daisy and even my now sporadic contact with her. And when Daisy landed on my doorstep one windy afternoon in tears, three months after telling me about her forthcoming nuptials, Karen welcomed her in and we sat together, drinking wine and mulling over Daisy's fear of committing to Bradley.

When she finally left in the early hours of the morning, I walked her to her car. She turned to me and put her arms around me. I hugged her softly and let her go. I couldn't let myself feel so drawn to her again and being in her presence all evening, as relaxing as it was, was somewhat disconcerting. I kept wondering what if … and I knew it was not healthy to do that.

She let me go and looked up at me. I remember those intense eyes staring into mine. "You know, Derek, I always hoped you might ride into town on your big black horse and rescue me."

"Are you okay, Daisy? Are you sure you want to go through with it?"

She nodded. "I do love him."

"I'm always here," I said and watched as she drove away, knowing in my heart she was never going to be happy with Bradley.

I walked into the house. Karen had already gotten into bed and I crept in beside her. I put my arms around her, knowing I was in love with her.

"She's still in love with you, you know."

"Hey, Karen," I said suddenly. "Will you marry me?"

****

I met Daisy for coffee around two months before my wedding. She stopped into town to see her family and asked if I would like to catch up.

"Congratulations," I said, genuinely happy for her but I could see she wasn't the same vibrant Daisy I had seen some six months earlier. "How are things?" Even though we'd continued talking on the phone, the calls were few and far between without mention of anything meaningful.

"Brad's good. I'm good," she replied and plastered a fake smile on her face.

"Want to talk about it?" The tears fell like an open tap, down her cheeks, over that perfect mouth. I put my hand on her arm. "Hey, hey," I said in what I thought was a soothing tone.

"I'm not happy, Derek," she blurted. "I don't know if I can ever be happy being married to a man who, as wonderful as he is, is literally … a farmer."

"But …"

"I rushed it, Derek. I moved so quickly. I think it was to make my parents happy. My mum was sick and I knew it would make her happy before she passed away. But I think I jumped into it without thinking it through."

"But you love him, don't you?"

She nodded slowly. Then she looked up at me. "Are you certain about Karen?"

I was taken aback. "What do you mean?"

"I would leave him, Derek. If you are not certain about Karen, I would leave him, come back here, come back to you."

"I love Karen," I said, my heart breaking for Daisy but knowing we couldn't go back to what we were.

Daisy nodded and bared her teeth in a smile. "I'm happy for you, Derek." I knew she put on a brave face for me and I appreciated that she didn't try to tear me apart.

And Karen and I were married.

And three years later, Karen left me. It was fairly amicable but I was hurt for a long time.

I wondered about Daisy. After that meeting, our communication had fallen apart. I think we both knew we had to keep apart if our marriages were to survive.

I started to think about Daisy again. Where was she now? How was she doing? Would it be okay to check on her? Yes, selfish me, suddenly going back to what was always there, unable to be there for her while I was married, not thinking about how she may feel about me contacting her again.

When she answered her phone, her tone was elated; it was clear she was happy to hear my voice. She had a second child on the way but she was still dissatisfied in her marriage. I felt certain that we could still be friends though, talking and writing, and we kept in touch, sharing our lives with each other via phone calls and text messages. We never saw each other face to face. There was no opportunity and neither of us talked about doing so. I think we knew it would be dangerous especially as I was now a single man.

A year later, I moved to Melbourne. The break-up with Karen had taken its toll and I needed a change, something drastic. I got myself a job in a Catholic school and there I met Marisa. I fell in love with Marisa instantly and we were married six months after our first date. Marisa was beautiful, fun and, like Karen, shared the same interests, values and goals as I did. She was the best thing that happened to me and we started our life together. Life with Marisa was fantastic. I loved her with every inch of me and we had two beautiful boys, kind and vivacious like their mum, outgoing and smart like me.

I kept in touch with Daisy and one week in 2012, Daisy and her children came to Melbourne without Bradley, and we all had a lovely time together, our children getting along well. But I caught her watching as Marisa and I worked together around the kitchen getting dinner ready, watching the ease and love with which we worked together. I saw her envy, her awe. I knew she wasn't happy. When she left, I hoped she could be as happy as I was with Marisa.

Then one day, I got a call from Daisy. She was in tears. "He said we can't talk or communicate anymore," she cried.

"Why?" I knew why. She had never told Bradley that she was in contact with me.

"He found our messages ..."

"But there's nothing weird in them."

"It doesn't matter," she said. "Just the fact that I told you I was unhappy, that I talk to you the way I do."

"Then maybe we shouldn't anymore," I said.

"But you're a big part of my life."

"And he is your husband," I said.

"And I have broken his heart," she said softly.

"Goodbye, Daisy," I said with sorrow. I wanted her in my life but I couldn't do anything for her. She had chosen to marry Bradley and I couldn't get in the way of a chance to be happy. I couldn't be her crutch anymore.

****

It was my fiftieth birthday and I was sending invites to a number of people from my past and I thought about Daisy. By now my marriage with Marisa was done. Nothing particular, no cheating on either part, but we grew apart and even though we tried to make it work, we knew we had to end it. I was heartbroken but we remained close and she even helped to organise my party.

So I included Daisy in the invitations that I sent out.

Who is this? was the reply.

Sorry, I must have messed up the number, I texted back. Maybe she had a different number now. It had been a few years since we'd been in contact.

The next day, I received another text from Daisy's number. *This is Daisy's daughter. Should I tell my mum that you messaged?*

I knew better than to mess up her life any more than I probably had already.

Daisy and I had been connected from day one, the moment I laid eyes on her, with her subtle beauty, her helpless countenance. There was no one who had been such a constant in my life, someone, who, I regret to say, I relied on. Our chemistry was the thing that kept us coming back together, but I knew I had to move on with my life without her in it.

I didn't reply and blocked the number.

Deana and Javier - *One Moment*

Bonus story!

There is a connection. You feel it and you know he does too.

It's an icy Sunday morning and I'm running. I need to run to keep my body lithe. The years take their toll; the kilos that dropped off so easily before are harder to shed and I've never had an easy time keeping them off in any case. A good diet and keeping my body moving helps to keep me looking younger than my forty years.

Forty. That's an acute number. Life begins at forty, isn't that what they say? I don't know who really says that but I think it's supposed to mean that the fun years have gone by and life becomes hard. Maybe it means that the good times have begun. I don't know which I prefer but now that I've hit forty, perhaps I'll opt for the latter.

Bon Jovi is rocking my earphones and I'm humming along, bouncing to the beat. The sun is trying to peep out from the clouds and I know it's going to be a good day. For once, I don't have much planned. Harry is taking the boys to a birthday party and leaving me some time to pamper myself. I smile when I think of Harry. We've been through a lot, Harry and I. Life is tough, but with Harry by my side, it's worth it. I work four days a week now the boys are both at school but it's still exhausting. It doesn't end. Marriage has its ups and downs, I guess, but we almost didn't make it. The bills at the beginning almost tore us apart and Harry's job as a machinist didn't cover them. But we worked through it. I worked part time while I studied to be a nurse and after a while things got better. Then the kids came along and took every ounce of energy from us both.

Harry is a great father. I knew it when I met him, that he would be. You could see it in the way he held my hand, so gently, how he held on to the small of my back when we walked into a room, how he opened car doors for me. He still does that and I know it's seen as sexist or something, but it's what it means that matters. That he still puts me first.

No, it's not the same as it was when we first met but I don't think it's supposed to be. We work together and yes, the passion that once was may have waned but what we have now is so much more than that.

I miss that spark sometimes, yearn for it, but it's hard to try to reignite that when you're so much more connected than just by the sliver of a flame.

I smile at the thought of Harry and return to the thought of what I might pamper myself with on the only day in a few months that I have a moment on my own. Maybe I'll take a long bath, maybe curl up with a book. I may go out and get a manicure. I look down at my nails and notice that the shoelace on my jogger is undone.

I stop beside a bench and rest my foot on it. It is next to a lake, one which I've been circling, and I notice a shadow fall over the seat. I don't look up but I get a slight shiver. Maybe it's the idea that I thought I was alone, maybe it's because I'm alone. The shadow remains and I focus on Jon Bon Jovi's voice belting out a love song, one of my favourites. It's annoying that I can't enjoy it, not with this sudden interference in my routine.

The shadow moves a little bit and I pull at the ends of the tied laces and swing around, ready to face this intruder of my peace.

All I see are eyes, deep blue, penetrating blue. He's saying something but I can't make out what and I lean forward. He flashes his brilliant white teeth at me and I realise that I still have my earphones in. I take them out hurriedly.

"Sorry, didn't hear you."

"No, I didn't think you could." He has a slight accent, French, maybe Spanish? But his voice is deep. It gives me the wobbles and I put my foot down to regain my balance. Suddenly I want to talk to him, to keep him talking. He's tall, his hair is a little wavy, dark.

"I'm Deana," I say and reach out my hand to him. It's an odd thing to do. I don't know what he wants.

"Javier," he says, taking my hand and letting his linger in mine for longer than the usual introductory handshake. "It's turning out to be a pleasant day," he says.

"It's going to be beautiful," I say, not knowing where this conversation is leading. I stretch, mainly for something to do.

"I like Sydney," he says.

"I love it here," I say, moving my body to the side.

"You are very fit," he says, his eyes wandering to my legs. I'm pleased. More than pleased. My workouts are paying off.

"You look fit too," I reply. What a stupid reply but I do admire the way his t-shirt falls over his torso, sticking to his abs. My eyes dart back up to his eyes. I've let my eyes wander for too long and when my eyes meet his, they are in a smile, little creases at the ends of them. I'm taking him to be younger than me, maybe thirty-ish?

There's an awkward silence and I turn to the water, looking at the ripples made by the morning swans as they glide across the lake. It's one of my favourite times of the day but I want to look back at him. There's something weird going on. My heart is hammering and I want to remain with this stranger longer.

"Deana," he says hesitantly and I look back at him. There's something there too. I can feel it.

"Yes?"

"What would you say if I asked you if you're free tonight?"

I want to forget my life for a night. I want to feel this, the buzz , the crazy feeling that's rumpling my tummy, making my fingers shake. The little tremor that is moving up my legs. It's been too long since I felt this, this euphoria — better than any drug, I imagine. He is looking at me expectantly. I haven't given him an answer and every bad thing in me wants to accept, just for the heck of it.

"I would say, Javier, that I'm a married woman with two children. A happily married woman."

His eyes drop for a quick second and then he looks into my eyes again, a reluctant smile hitting his lips. "Good for you, Deana. Lucky man." He holds out his hand and I put mine in it. He raises it to his mouth and I feel tingles as his lips graze my knuckles. He drops it and turns to leave. "By the way," he says with a lopsided smile. "You dropped this." He hands me my house keys, two little keys on a ring.

I take them, happy to get a touch of his hand on mine again as he gives them to me.

I am left gaping, my mouth ajar as he turns and jogs away. That feeling is strong still; what it is, is still with me. I swallow hard and turn to go home. To my life, my beautiful life.

Will I ever see him again? I don't know. Do I want to? No, I don't. That moment is enough.

Acknowledgements

My contributors, first and foremost, the named and the unnamed.

Michael Patchell, Olivia Reljic, Michael Cooper, Kipp Roane and the anonymous contributors, thank you for the time and effort you have poured into these stories. I know for some of you this was an arduous task, bringing up memories that you would prefer had been left buried. For you to unearth these memories for my sake means the absolute world to me and I just hope that I have done your stories justice.

Thank you to my betas, Kerrie Hall, Tina Krog, Heidi L, Julia Kalman and Julie Parry-Barwick. And a shout-out to my editor, always ready to read my work— Anita.

Thank you to my fam, as usual, for their input, for just making me love life, really.

To all the Billys out there in the world, thank you! And just remember, we ourselves may be somebody's Billy.

ABOUT THE AUTHOR

Rita H Rowe is a teacher and author with a Bachelor of Arts, a Diploma of Education, and a Masters in Writing. Her journey into writing began as a lifelong dream that she was finally able to pursue at the age of forty-seven, resulting in her first novel, Never the Moon. Rita pours her heart and soul into her writing, incorporating her personal experiences with love, romance, hurt, and abuse. To Rita, writing is both a form of therapy and a way to connect with like-minded readers on a deeper level. As an author, Rita hopes to be remembered as someone who created worlds that readers could lose themselves in, even just for a little while. When she isn't writing, Rita enjoys playing pool, painting, going on motorbike rides, and spending time with her children and mother.

Other Novels by Rita H Rowe

NEVER THE MOON

Two men who could not be more different.

One woman caught between them.

When Jennifer loses David, the love of her life, her world falls apart. Fleeing to New York for a fresh start, she meets Jack, rugged and handsome, everything she could hope for.

But her world is unexpectedly plunged into chaos and violence.

An abusive husband, a loveless marriage - and no way out.

When David comes back into her life; Jennifer is torn between the man she has always loved and a life she has now chosen...

Never The Moon interweaves the lives of Jennifer, David and Jack, revealing the power of love - and the destruction it can leave in   its   wake...

"Inspired and emotive, a great romance and heart-string tugger of a story...well done to a new voice of romance..." Debra, Indiebook reviewer.

SHE REMEMBERED

Her beauty is a curse. Her memories a void. Elena cannot remember. All she has are fragments of a past life that feel foreign to her, only glimpsed in fleeting moments through violent nightmares. Struggling to put her life together and find acceptance, she takes comfort in Luke, a charming boy who seems to like her as much as she likes him. But nothing has ever come easily to Elena — and when she wakes up between blood-soaked sheets next to the body of a man recently stabbed, what little stability she had comes crashing down around her.

With no one to help her and nowhere to go, Elena has to salvage the broken pieces of her life all on her own. If only she could remember …

"I didn't predict the outcome and I thoroughly enjoyed the journey to get there. Definitely 5 stars from me." Umm Ibrahim – Amazon.

DANCING WITH GHOSTS

Alex will never dance again. Her parents and her dreams, all lost in one fateful night. Unable to put her faith in love and happiness, not even for Nicholas, the man she loves, she escapes to Chernut, a country town far from the reminders of her past. Here at the beautiful Lovelet Manor, inhabited by a family who are as lost as she is, Alex finds solace in the picturesque gardens of which she is caretaker, accepting that her life can never be full again. But when she meets Edward in the grand gazebo, she discovers that her heart may not be done with her yet. And for the first time in a long time, she allows herself to be loved.

But is she losing her mind? Will the ghosts of her past keep her running forever? Or will Alex find herself before she runs out of time?

"Binge worthy. This is a ghost story with romance and characters so very real they are believable. I loved it." Amazon reviewer.

THE BAD SEED

Love, betrayal and murder. He's the new kid in town, complete with a sordid past and a tarnished family name, doomed to fail even before he begins. Jenna is the only person who sees beyond Joey's past and they fall deeply in love. But there are already forces determined to separate the pair by any means necessary. Tommy, the thug, who is hell-bent on breaking Joey by brute force, Jenna's mother, whose connection with Joey cannot be ignored, and Joey's own past, the strongest weapon against them. Only Tim, the local police officer, shows any compassion to the plight of Joey and Jenna, but is Tim all he seems? And what role will he play in their fate? Can young love survive in a town filled with discrimination?
Can Joey and Jenna get out before they fall apart, or is it already too late?

"A thrilling, heartbreaking read. I finished this book four days ago and I still can't get it out of my mind." Tina MK, Amazon.

BECOMING RUTHLESS

When all the men she knows are liars, maybe it's time to become one too.
Ruth is young, excited about life and not looking for love. Yet love finds her, and Ruth is thrilled. But she is left devastated when she finds out that her the man she loves has deceived her. Still hopeful, she embarks on another relationship only to find herself in the same predicament. Ruth becomes disenchanted with love and decides that if she can't beat them, she may as well join them and begins a journey that will change her very being and endanger her life.
Can Ruth find herself before it's too late? Or will she become what she has always despised — a loathsome liar?

"When I tell you I was excited for this book, I'm not kidding! I read it in one sitting, and absolutely could not put it down." *Rebecca, Amazon.*

THE IMPOSSIBLE CHOICE

Mary, still reeling from the loss of her husband, is living a quiet life, running a boarding house in the seaside town of Righteous Creek, her only priorities her two teenage daughters.

But the tranquillity in which she lives is about to be rocked with the appearance of Lawrence, ten years younger and with demons of his own.

And there is more at stake than just a love that cannot be fulfilled. Just when Mary defies her heart, her world is turned upside down again and she is left to make an unthinkable decision, an impossible choice.

"The rollercoaster of emotions that Ms Rowe manages to evoke in each one of her books is astounding and this novel is no exception. A little gem of a book with a conclusion that you will never see coming." Amazon Reviewer.

ALMOST HAPPY

Meet Beverley: she's timid, shy, struggles in social settings and has health problems that prevent her from living life to the full. She is, however, appreciative of the things she does have, a bond with her sister, Dina, who is so different from her, and the love of Troy, her childhood sweetheart who may be caring, but can also be controlling.

When Troy leaves her, Beverley feels free. She meets Jay, thoughtful and unlike any love she has ever felt before, and a lifetime of happiness beckons. But when Jay abandons her unexpectedly, she feels like her world has fallen apart.

Troy is never far away, and when he returns to Beverley's life and asks for her hand in marriage, she accepts, realising that it's better to be almost happy than not at all. But these slivers of happiness are threatened when Jay returns, bringing with him secrets that could destroy her world. A world that is so carefully held together with hope.

How can Beverley ignore the betrayal that has torn apart every fabric of her life? How can she leave everything she loves, so she can finally be free?

"Oh wow what can I say? For the first couple of chapters I wondered if I was going to get into this one but then it hit me and I was completely absorbed. This novel is strikingly sad if you look deeply into it but comes across as only tinged with sadness. The theme of emotional abuse and threatening behaviour may be hard for some to read but I felt it was handled well and made for an enjoyable read. For me it had vibes of "never the moon" by the same author so if you enjoyed that, I feel you would love this too." Amazon Reviewer.

IT'S JUST CHEMISTRY

Is it love, or is it just chemistry? Fiona and Danny are about to find out.

They say opposites attract, and that is true with Danny and Fiona. He is athletic and the star of the soccer team. She is a dreamer and the star of the stage. Sparks fly when they meet and fall in love.

But can you stay together when you have differences as significant as they do? Their love for each other is immense, but so is the jealousy that comes with such great love. After three tumultuous years, Fiona is faced with the ultimate betrayal that will see her wipe Danny out of her life forever.

Fate, however, has other ideas and keeps drawing them back together. But how can two people who are so different, so unwavering in their life choices, be together when their lives are so far apart?

What is it that pulls them together time and time again?

Is it something deeper, or is it just chemistry?

Follow Rita H Rowe on Facebook or Instagram or visit her website www.ritahrowe.com. Leave a review or drop her a line. She loves to hear from her readers.

www.ingramcontent.com/pod-product-compliance
Lightning Source LLC
Chambersburg PA
CBHW020411150626
46554CB00013B/697